W9-BXV-473

GOSCINNY AND UDERZO
PRESENT
An Asterix Adventure

ASTERIX
AND THE
CHIEFTAIN'S SHIELD

Written by RENÉ GOSCINNY *and Illustrated by* ALBERT UDERZO

Translated by Anthea Bell *and* Derek Hockridge

© 1968 GOSCINNY/UDERZO

Revised edition and English translation © 2004 HACHETTE

Original title: *Le Bouclier Arverne*

Exclusive licensee: Orion Publishing Group
Translators: Anthea Bell and Derek Hockridge
Typography: Bryony Newhouse

All rights reserved

The right of René Goscinny and Albert Uderzo to be identified as the authors of this work
have been asssserted by them in accordance with the Copyright, Designs and Patents Act 1988.

This revised edition first published in 2004 by Orion Books Ltd,
Orion House, 5 Upper Saint Martin's Lane, London WC2H 9EA

3 5 7 9 10 8 6 4 2

Printed in France by Qualibris

http://gb.asterix.com
www.orionbooks.co.uk

A CIP record for this book is available from the British Library

ISBN-13 978 0 75286 624 6 (cased)
ISBN-10 0 75286 624 9 (cased)
ISBN-13 978 0 75286 625 3 (paperback)
ISBN-10 0 75286 625 7 (paperback)

Distributed in the United States of America by Sterling Publishing Co. Inc.
387 Park Avenue South, New York, NY 10016

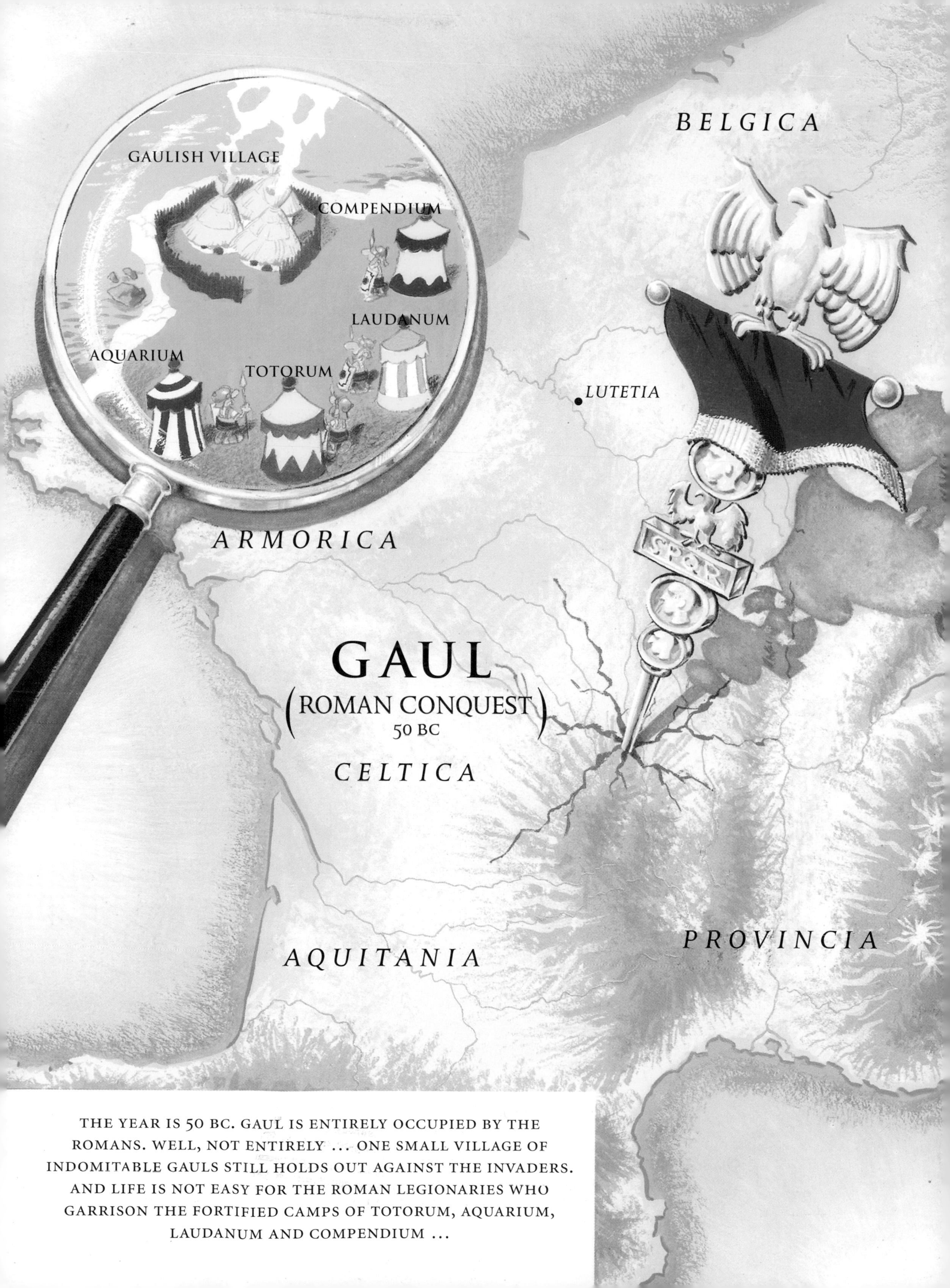
BELGICA
GAULISH VILLAGE
COMPENDIUM
LAUDANUM
AQUARIUM
TOTORUM
LUTETIA
SPQR
ARMORICA
GAUL
(ROMAN CONQUEST)
50 BC
CELTICA
AQUITANIA
PROVINCIA

THE YEAR IS 50 BC. GAUL IS ENTIRELY OCCUPIED BY THE ROMANS. WELL, NOT ENTIRELY ... ONE SMALL VILLAGE OF INDOMITABLE GAULS STILL HOLDS OUT AGAINST THE INVADERS. AND LIFE IS NOT EASY FOR THE ROMAN LEGIONARIES WHO GARRISON THE FORTIFIED CAMPS OF TOTORUM, AQUARIUM, LAUDANUM AND COMPENDIUM ...

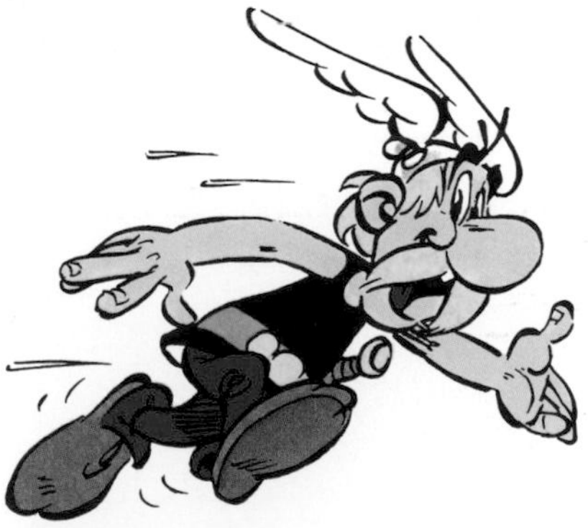

ASTERIX, THE HERO OF THESE ADVENTURES. A SHREWD, CUNNING LITTLE WARRIOR, ALL PERILOUS MISSIONS ARE IMMEDIATELY ENTRUSTED TO HIM. ASTERIX GETS HIS SUPERHUMAN STRENGTH FROM THE MAGIC POTION BREWED BY THE DRUID GETAFIX . . .

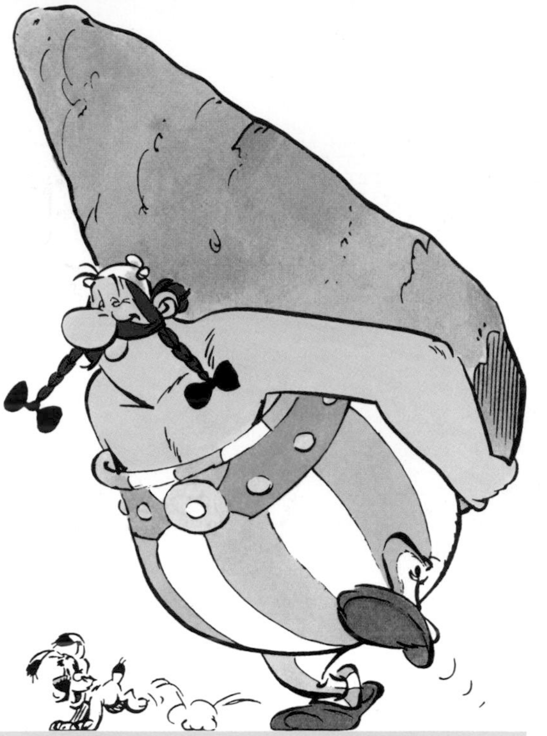

OBELIX, ASTERIX'S INSEPARABLE FRIEND. A MENHIR DELIVERY MAN BY TRADE, ADDICTED TO WILD BOAR. OBELIX IS ALWAYS READY TO DROP EVERYTHING AND GO OFF ON A NEW ADVENTURE WITH ASTERIX – SO LONG AS THERE'S WILD BOAR TO EAT, AND PLENTY OF FIGHTING. HIS CONSTANT COMPANION IS DOGMATIX, THE ONLY KNOWN CANINE ECOLOGIST, WHO HOWLS WITH DESPAIR WHEN A TREE IS CUT DOWN.

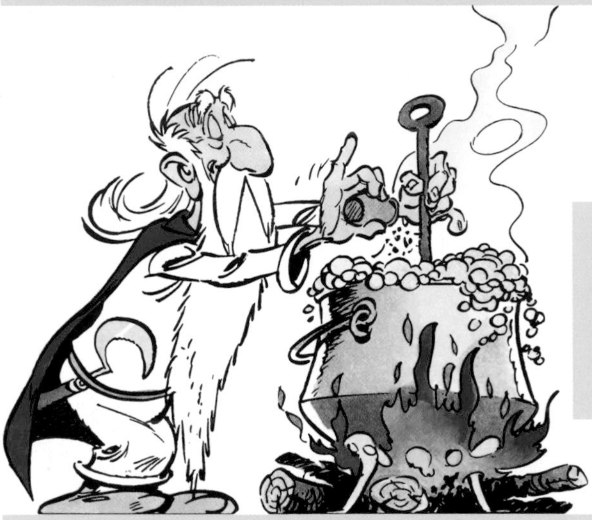

GETAFIX, THE VENERABLE VILLAGE DRUID, GATHERS MISTLETOE AND BREWS MAGIC POTIONS. HIS SPECIALITY IS THE POTION WHICH GIVES THE DRINKER SUPERHUMAN STRENGTH. BUT GETAFIX ALSO HAS OTHER RECIPES UP HIS SLEEVE . . .

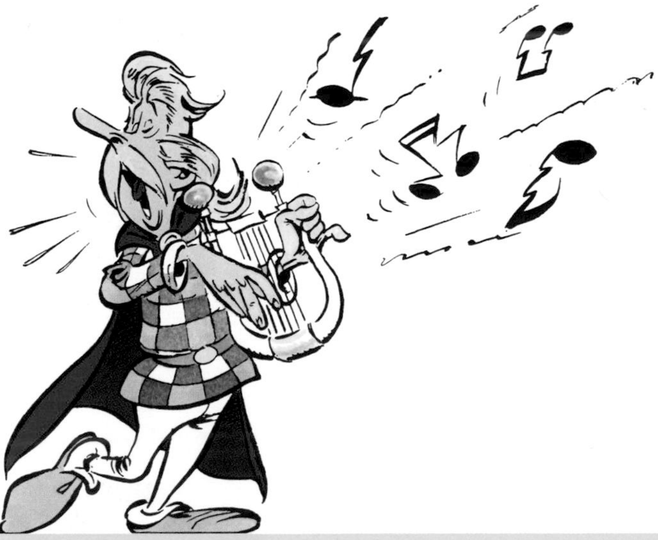

CACOFONIX, THE BARD. OPINION IS DIVIDED AS TO HIS MUSICAL GIFTS. CACOFONIX THINKS HE'S A GENIUS. EVERYONE ELSE THINKS HE'S UNSPEAKABLE. BUT SO LONG AS HE DOESN'T SPEAK, LET ALONE SING, EVERYBODY LIKES HIM . . .

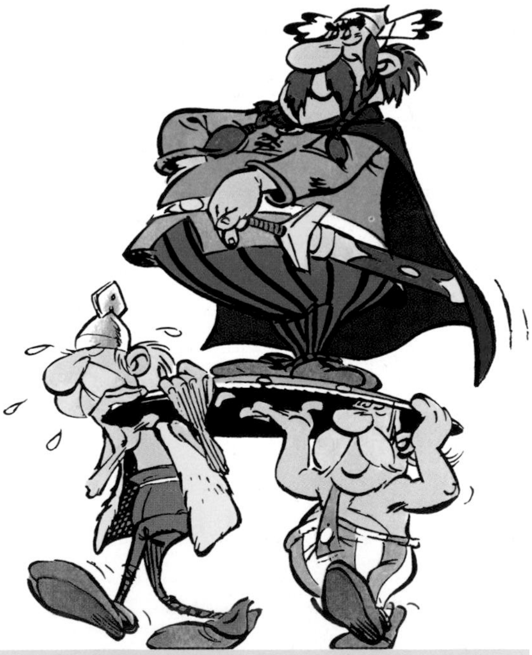

FINALLY, VITALSTATISTIX, THE CHIEF OF THE TRIBE. MAJESTIC, BRAVE AND HOT-TEMPERED, THE OLD WARRIOR IS RESPECTED BY HIS MEN AND FEARED BY HIS ENEMIES. VITALSTATISTIX HIMSELF HAS ONLY ONE FEAR, HE IS AFRAID THE SKY MAY FALL ON HIS HEAD TOMORROW. BUT AS HE ALWAYS SAYS, TOMORROW NEVER COMES.

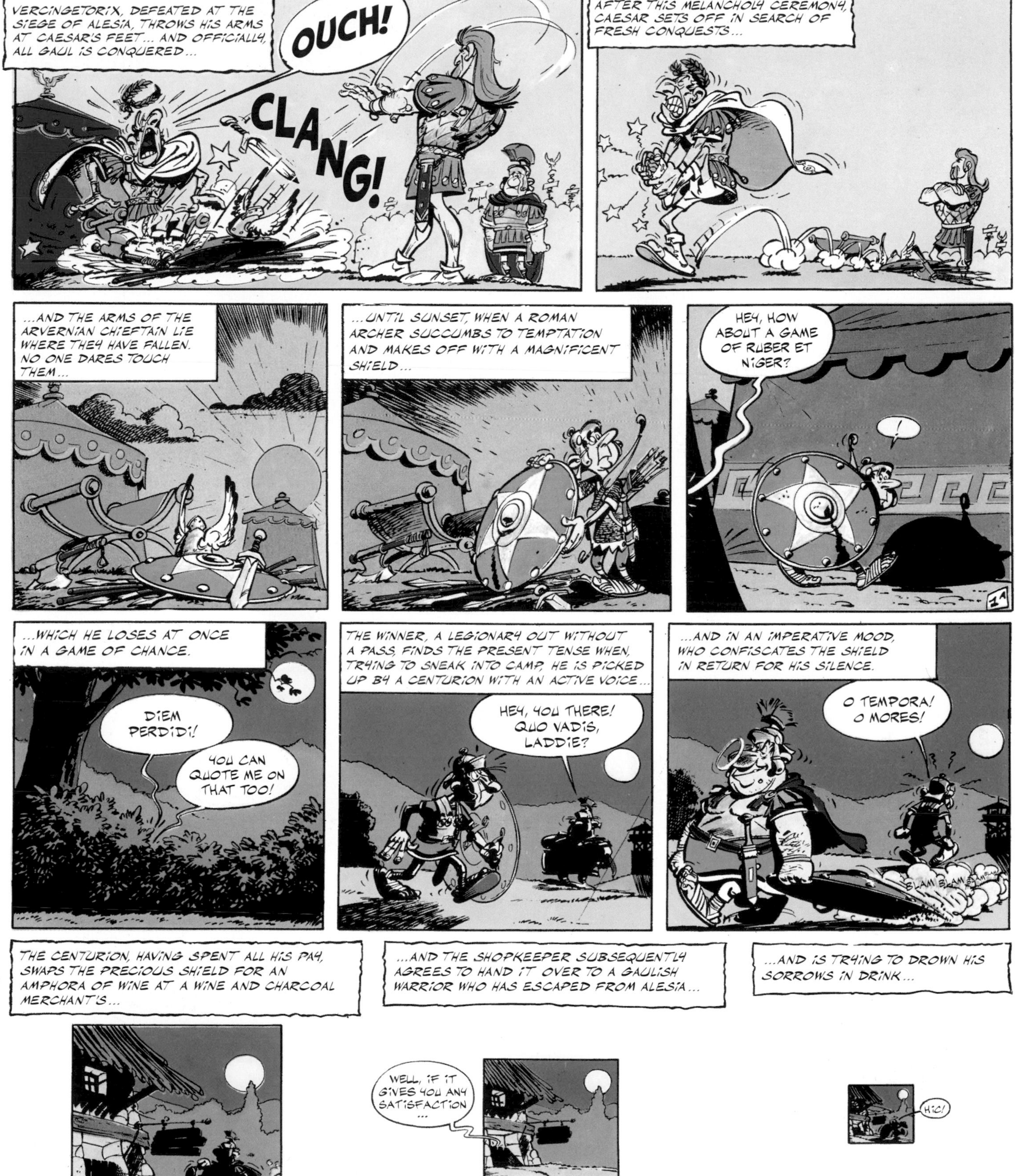
VERCINGETORIX, DEFEATED AT THE SIEGE OF ALESIA, THROWS HIS ARMS AT CAESAR'S FEET... AND OFFICIALLY, ALL GAUL IS CONQUERED...
OUCH!
CLANG!
AFTER THIS MELANCHOLY CEREMONY, CAESAR SETS OFF IN SEARCH OF FRESH CONQUESTS...
...AND THE ARMS OF THE ARVERNIAN CHIEFTAIN LIE WHERE THEY HAVE FALLEN. NO ONE DARES TOUCH THEM...
...UNTIL SUNSET, WHEN A ROMAN ARCHER SUCCUMBS TO TEMPTATION AND MAKES OFF WITH A MAGNIFICENT SHIELD...
HEY, HOW ABOUT A GAME OF RUBER ET NIGER?
!
...WHICH HE LOSES AT ONCE IN A GAME OF CHANCE.
DIEM PERDIDI!
YOU CAN QUOTE ME ON THAT TOO!
THE WINNER, A LEGIONARY OUT WITHOUT A PASS, FINDS THE PRESENT TENSE WHEN, TRYING TO SNEAK INTO CAMP, HE IS PICKED UP BY A CENTURION WITH AN ACTIVE VOICE...
HEY, YOU THERE! QUO VADIS, LADDIE?
...AND IN AN IMPERATIVE MOOD, WHO CONFISCATES THE SHIELD IN RETURN FOR HIS SILENCE.
O TEMPORA! O MORES!
BLAM BLAM BLAM
THE CENTURION, HAVING SPENT ALL HIS PAY, SWAPS THE PRECIOUS SHIELD FOR AN AMPHORA OF WINE AT A WINE AND CHARCOAL MERCHANT'S...
...AND THE SHOPKEEPER SUBSEQUENTLY AGREES TO HAND IT OVER TO A GAULISH WARRIOR WHO HAS ESCAPED FROM ALESIA...
WELL, IF IT GIVES YOU ANY SATISFACTION ...
...AND IS TRYING TO DROWN HIS SORROWS IN DRINK...
HIC!

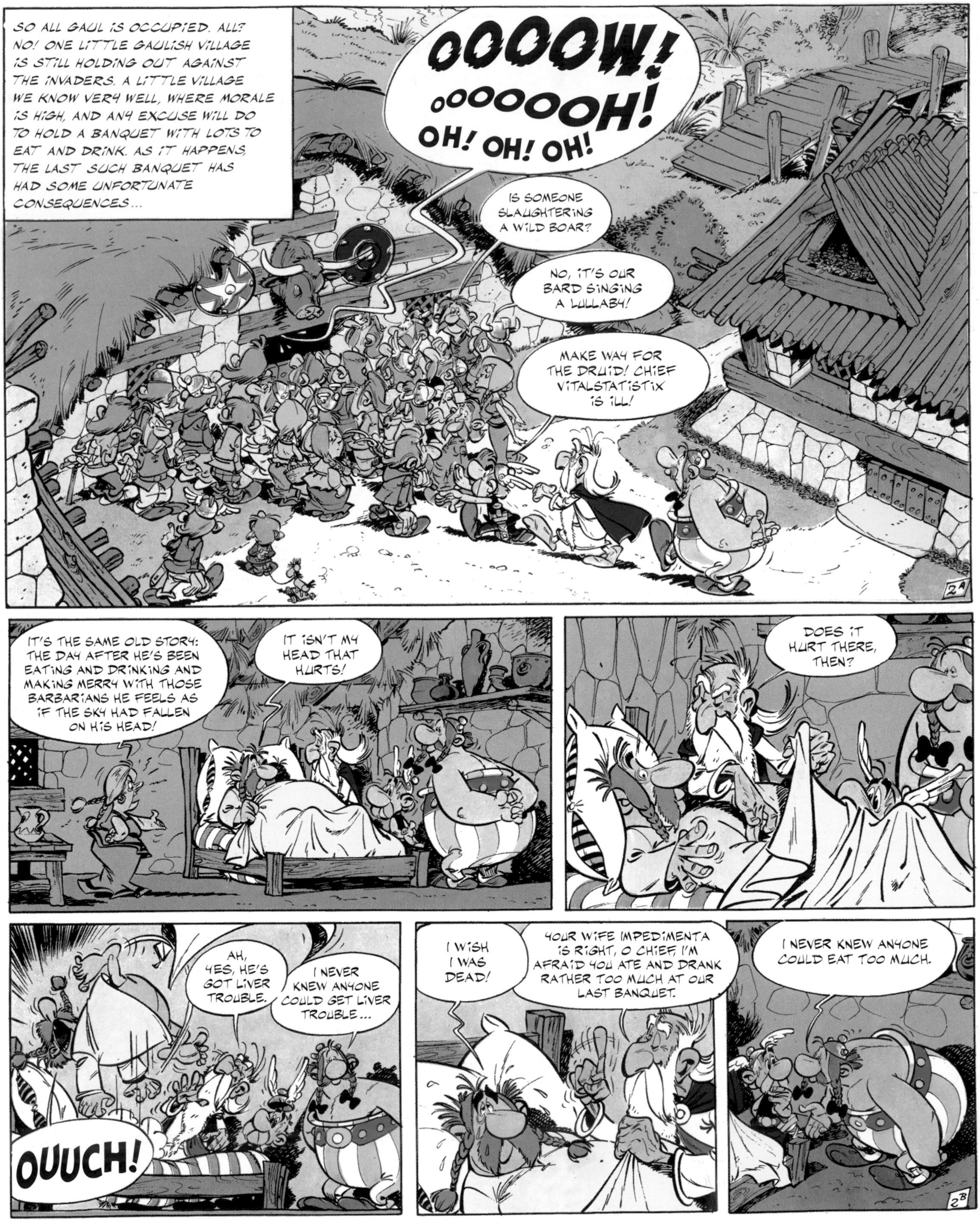
SO ALL GAUL IS OCCUPIED. ALL? NO! ONE LITTLE GAULISH VILLAGE IS STILL HOLDING OUT AGAINST THE INVADERS. A LITTLE VILLAGE WE KNOW VERY WELL, WHERE MORALE IS HIGH, AND ANY EXCUSE WILL DO TO HOLD A BANQUET WITH LOTS TO EAT AND DRINK. AS IT HAPPENS, THE LAST SUCH BANQUET HAS HAD SOME UNFORTUNATE CONSEQUENCES...
OOOOW! OOOOOOH! OH! OH! OH!
IS SOMEONE SLAUGHTERING A WILD BOAR?
NO, IT'S OUR BARD SINGING A LULLABY!
MAKE WAY FOR THE DRUID! CHIEF VITALSTATISTIX IS ILL!
IT'S THE SAME OLD STORY: THE DAY AFTER HE'S BEEN EATING AND DRINKING AND MAKING MERRY WITH THOSE BARBARIANS HE FEELS AS IF THE SKY HAD FALLEN ON HIS HEAD!
IT ISN'T MY HEAD THAT HURTS!
DOES IT HURT THERE, THEN?
OUUCH!
AH, YES, HE'S GOT LIVER TROUBLE.
I NEVER KNEW ANYONE COULD GET LIVER TROUBLE...
I WISH I WAS DEAD!
YOUR WIFE IMPEDIMENTA IS RIGHT, O CHIEF. I'M AFRAID YOU ATE AND DRANK RATHER TOO MUCH AT OUR LAST BANQUET.
I NEVER KNEW ANYONE COULD EAT TOO MUCH.

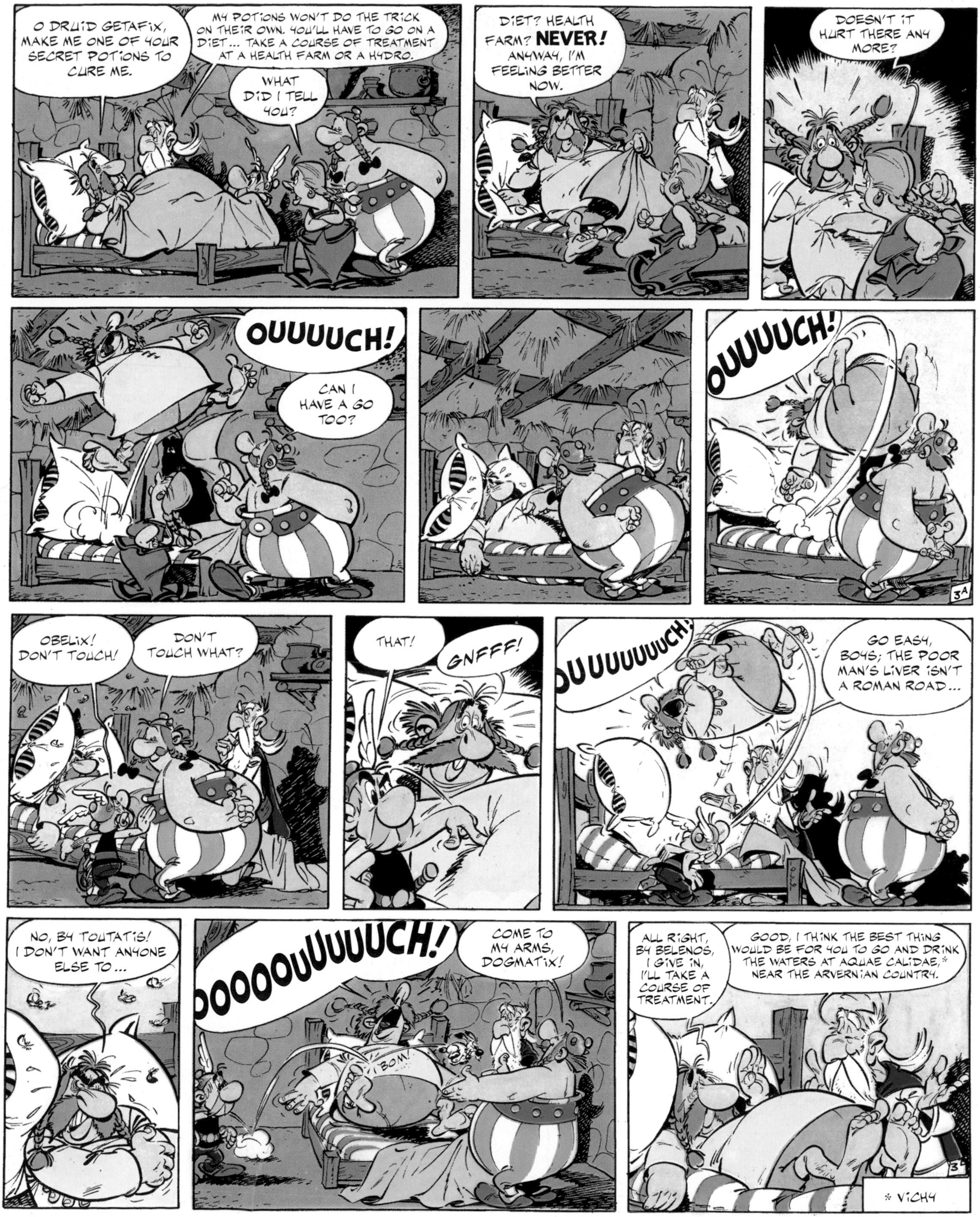

O DRUID GETAFIX, MAKE ME ONE OF YOUR SECRET POTIONS TO CURE ME.
MY POTIONS WON'T DO THE TRICK ON THEIR OWN. YOU'LL HAVE TO GO ON A DIET... TAKE A COURSE OF TREATMENT AT A HEALTH FARM OR A HYDRO.
WHAT DID I TELL YOU?
DIET? HEALTH FARM? NEVER! ANYWAY, I'M FEELING BETTER NOW.
DOESN'T IT HURT THERE ANY MORE?
OUUUUCH!
CAN I HAVE A GO TOO?
OUUUUCH!
OBELIX! DON'T TOUCH!
DON'T TOUCH WHAT?
THAT!
GNFFF!
OUUUUUUUCH!
GO EASY, BOYS; THE POOR MAN'S LIVER ISN'T A ROMAN ROAD...
NO, BY TOUTATIS! I DON'T WANT ANYONE ELSE TO...
OOOOOUUUUUCH!
COME TO MY ARMS, DOGMATIX!
BOM!
ALL RIGHT, BY BELENOS, I GIVE IN, I'LL TAKE A COURSE OF TREATMENT.
GOOD, I THINK THE BEST THING WOULD BE FOR YOU TO GO AND DRINK THE WATERS AT AQUAE CALIDAE,* NEAR THE ARVERNIAN COUNTRY.
* VICHY

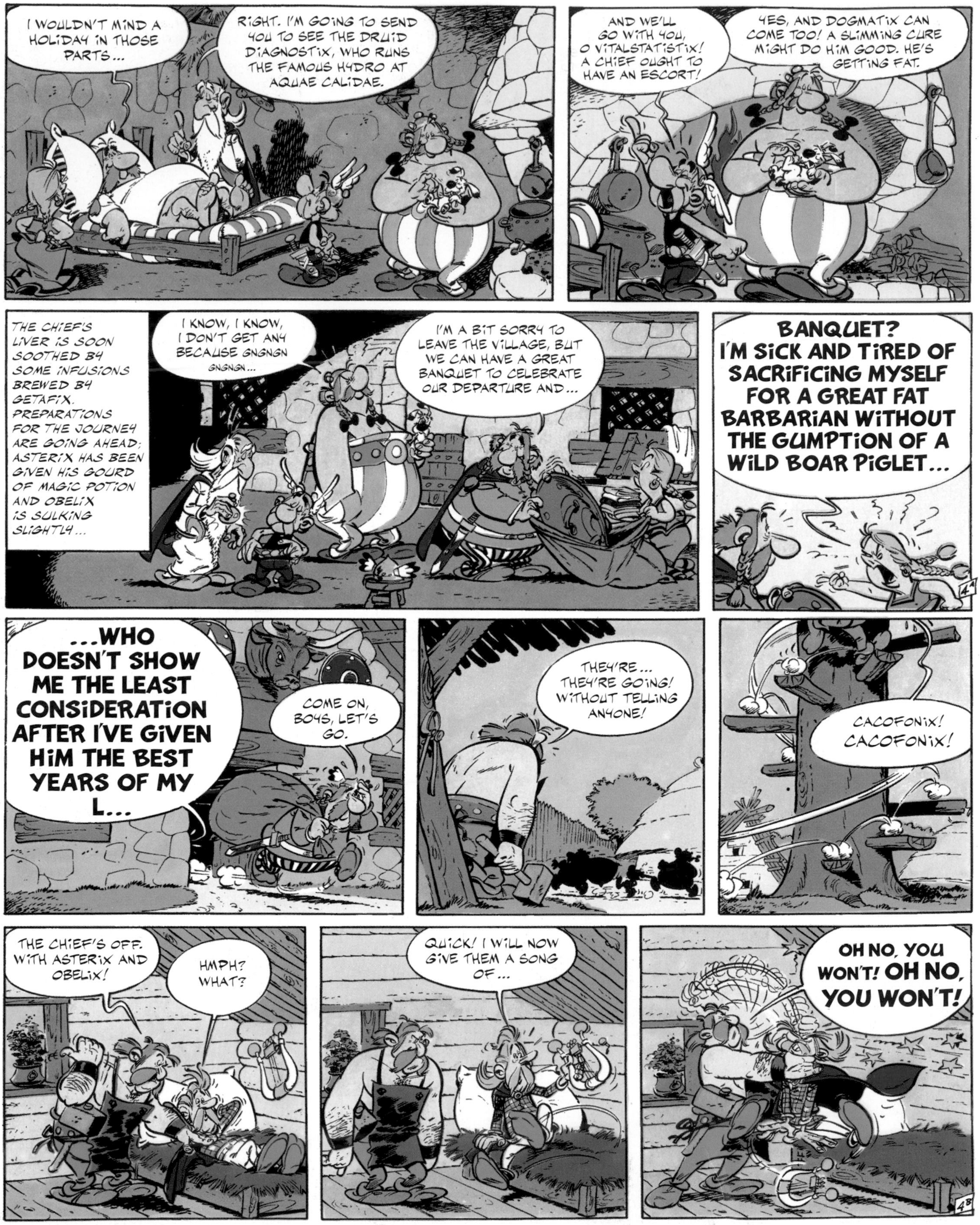
I WOULDN'T MIND A HOLIDAY IN THOSE PARTS...
RIGHT. I'M GOING TO SEND YOU TO SEE THE DRUID DIAGNOSTIX, WHO RUNS THE FAMOUS HYDRO AT AQUAE CALIDAE.
AND WE'LL GO WITH YOU, O VITALSTATISTIX! A CHIEF OUGHT TO HAVE AN ESCORT!
YES, AND DOGMATIX CAN COME TOO! A SLIMMING CURE MIGHT DO HIM GOOD. HE'S GETTING FAT.
THE CHIEF'S LIVER IS SOON SOOTHED BY SOME INFUSIONS BREWED BY GETAFIX. PREPARATIONS FOR THE JOURNEY ARE GOING AHEAD; ASTERIX HAS BEEN GIVEN HIS GOURD OF MAGIC POTION AND OBELIX IS SULKING SLIGHTLY...
I KNOW, I KNOW, I DON'T GET ANY BECAUSE GNGNGN GNGNGN...
I'M A BIT SORRY TO LEAVE THE VILLAGE, BUT WE CAN HAVE A GREAT BANQUET TO CELEBRATE OUR DEPARTURE AND...
BANQUET? I'M SICK AND TIRED OF SACRIFICING MYSELF FOR A GREAT FAT BARBARIAN WITHOUT THE GUMPTION OF A WILD BOAR PIGLET...
...WHO DOESN'T SHOW ME THE LEAST CONSIDERATION AFTER I'VE GIVEN HIM THE BEST YEARS OF MY L...
COME ON, BOYS, LET'S GO.
THEY'RE... THEY'RE GOING! WITHOUT TELLING ANYONE!
CACOFONIX! CACOFONIX!
THE CHIEF'S OFF. WITH ASTERIX AND OBELIX!
HMPH? WHAT?
QUICK! I WILL NOW GIVE THEM A SONG OF...
OH NO, YOU WON'T! OH NO, YOU WON'T!

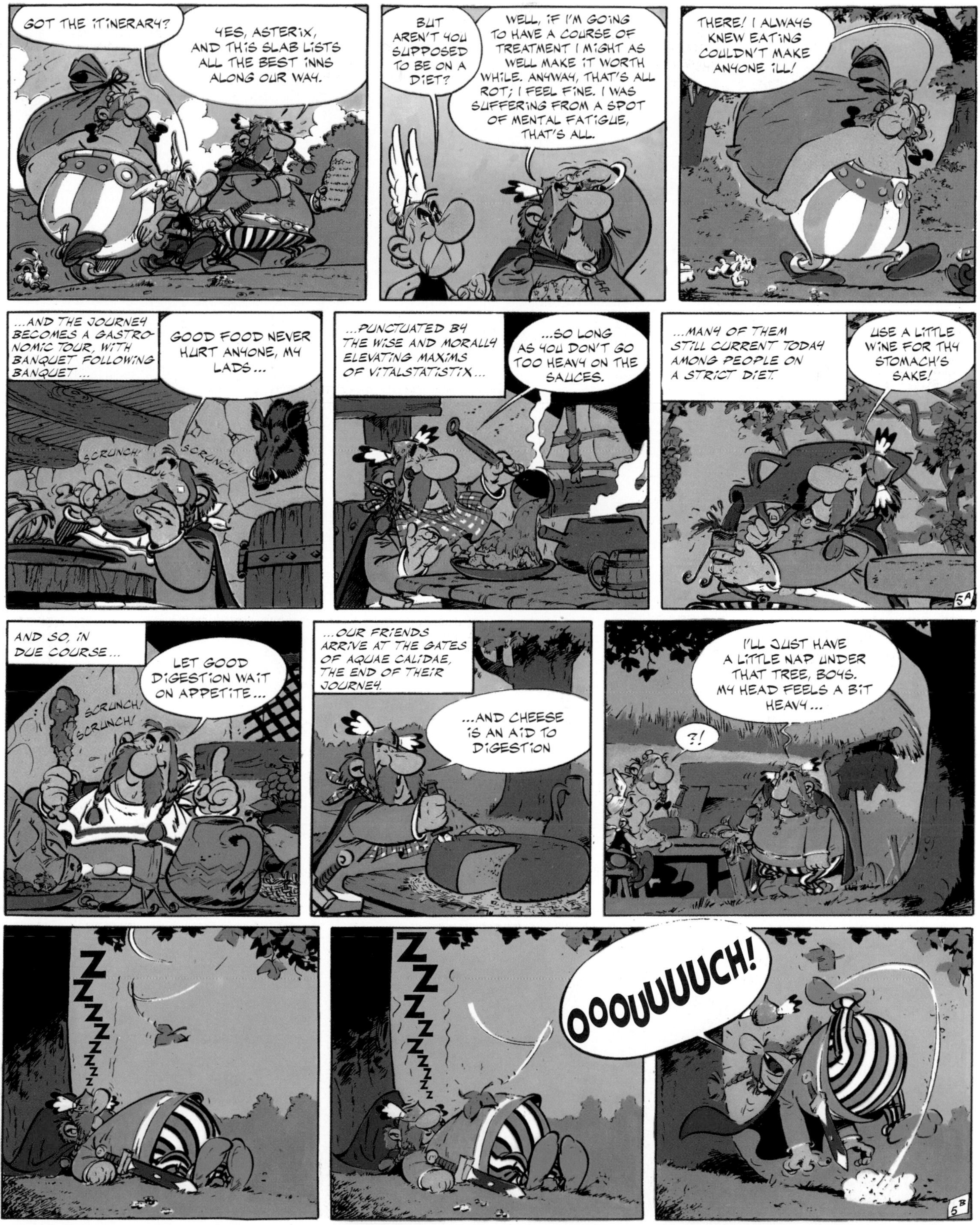
GOT THE ITINERARY?
YES, ASTERIX, AND THIS SLAB LISTS ALL THE BEST INNS ALONG OUR WAY.
BUT AREN'T YOU SUPPOSED TO BE ON A DIET?
WELL, IF I'M GOING TO HAVE A COURSE OF TREATMENT I MIGHT AS WELL MAKE IT WORTH WHILE. ANYWAY, THAT'S ALL ROT; I FEEL FINE. I WAS SUFFERING FROM A SPOT OF MENTAL FATIGUE, THAT'S ALL.
THERE! I ALWAYS KNEW EATING COULDN'T MAKE ANYONE ILL!
...AND THE JOURNEY BECOMES A GASTRONOMIC TOUR, WITH BANQUET FOLLOWING BANQUET...
GOOD FOOD NEVER HURT ANYONE, MY LADS...
SCRUNCH!
SCRUNCH!
...PUNCTUATED BY THE WISE AND MORALLY ELEVATING MAXIMS OF VITALSTATISTIX...
...SO LONG AS YOU DON'T GO TOO HEAVY ON THE SAUCES.
...MANY OF THEM STILL CURRENT TODAY AMONG PEOPLE ON A STRICT DIET.
USE A LITTLE WINE FOR THY STOMACH'S SAKE!
5A
AND SO, IN DUE COURSE...
LET GOOD DIGESTION WAIT ON APPETITE...
SCRUNCH! SCRUNCH!
...OUR FRIENDS ARRIVE AT THE GATES OF AQUAE CALIDAE, THE END OF THEIR JOURNEY.
...AND CHEESE IS AN AID TO DIGESTION
I'LL JUST HAVE A LITTLE NAP UNDER THAT TREE, BOYS. MY HEAD FEELS A BIT HEAVY...
?!
ZZZZZZZ
ZZZZZZZZ
OOOUUUUCH!
5B

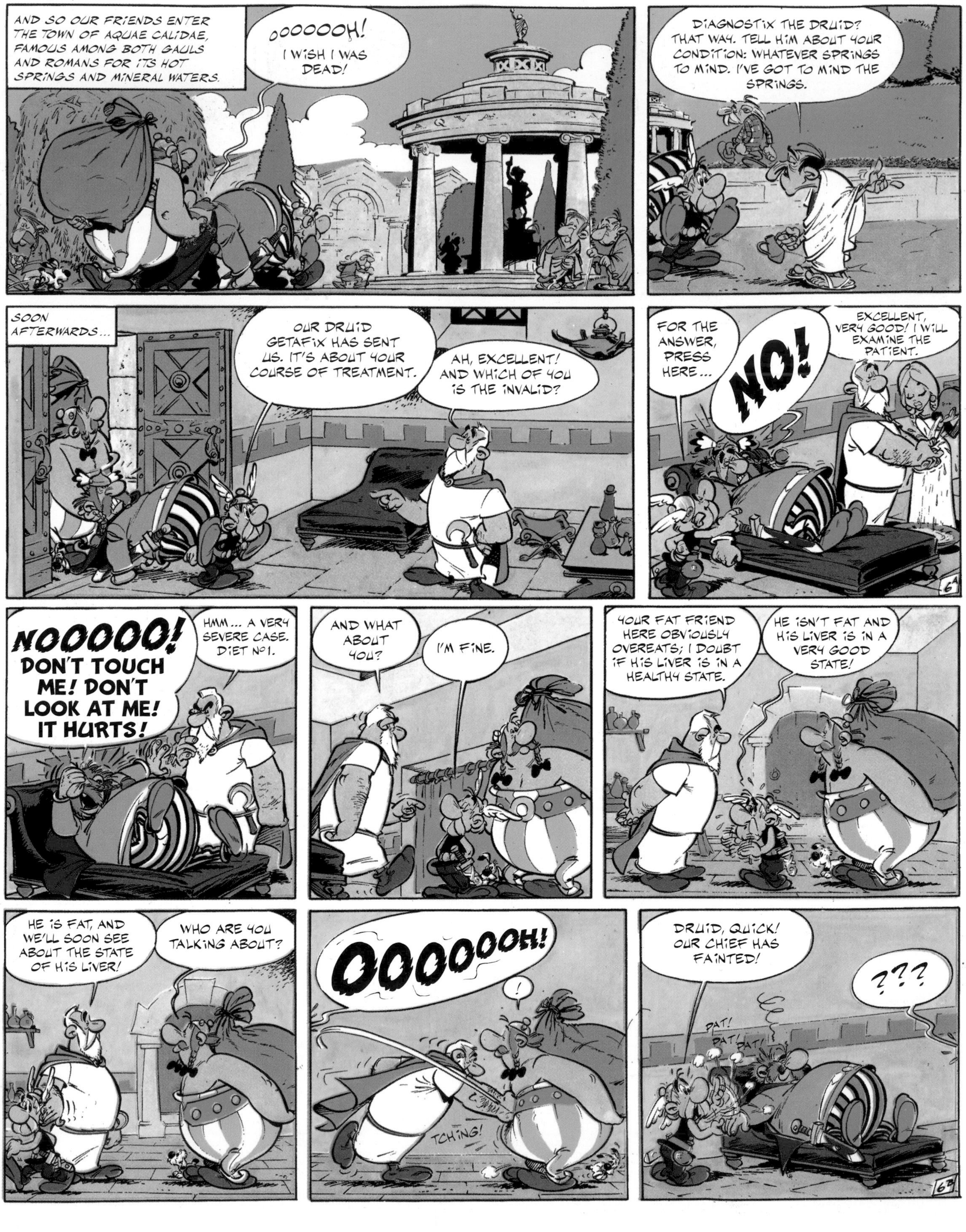
AND SO OUR FRIENDS ENTER THE TOWN OF AQUAE CALIDAE, FAMOUS AMONG BOTH GAULS AND ROMANS FOR ITS HOT SPRINGS AND MINERAL WATERS.
OOOOOOH! I WISH I WAS DEAD!
DIAGNOSTIX THE DRUID? THAT WAY. TELL HIM ABOUT YOUR CONDITION: WHATEVER SPRINGS TO MIND. I'VE GOT TO MIND THE SPRINGS.
SOON AFTERWARDS...
OUR DRUID GETAFIX HAS SENT US. IT'S ABOUT YOUR COURSE OF TREATMENT.
AH, EXCELLENT! AND WHICH OF YOU IS THE INVALID?
FOR THE ANSWER, PRESS HERE...
NO!
EXCELLENT, VERY GOOD! I WILL EXAMINE THE PATIENT.
NOOOOO! DON'T TOUCH ME! DON'T LOOK AT ME! IT HURTS!
HMM... A VERY SEVERE CASE. DIET No1.
AND WHAT ABOUT YOU?
I'M FINE.
YOUR FAT FRIEND HERE OBVIOUSLY OVEREATS; I DOUBT IF HIS LIVER IS IN A HEALTHY STATE.
HE ISN'T FAT AND HIS LIVER IS IN A VERY GOOD STATE!
HE IS FAT, AND WE'LL SOON SEE ABOUT THE STATE OF HIS LIVER!
WHO ARE YOU TALKING ABOUT?
OOOOOOH!
!
TCHING!
DRUID, QUICK! OUR CHIEF HAS FAINTED!
???
PAT! PAT! PAT!

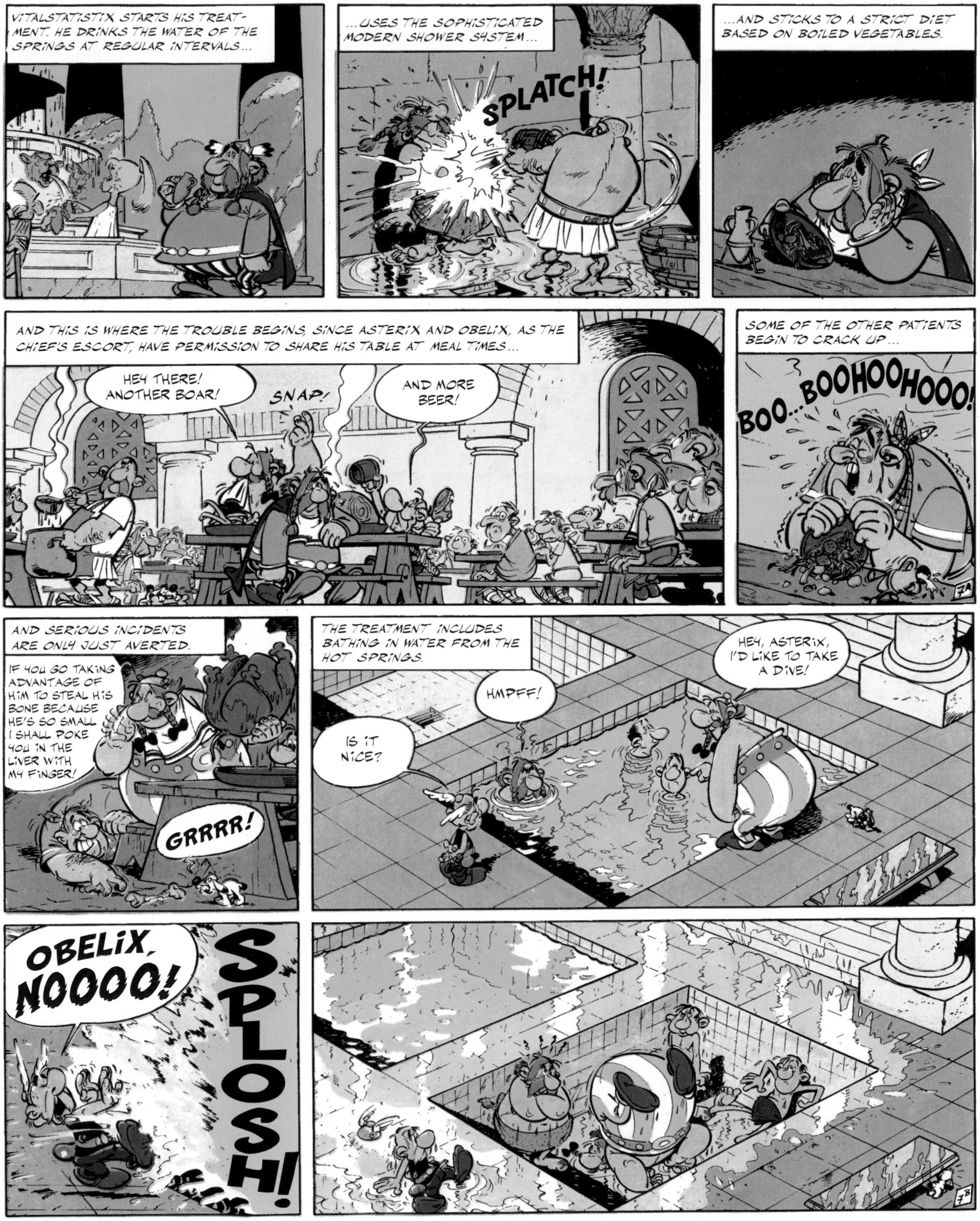
VITALSTATISTIX STARTS HIS TREATMENT. HE DRINKS THE WATER OF THE SPRINGS AT REGULAR INTERVALS...
...USES THE SOPHISTICATED MODERN SHOWER SYSTEM...
SPLATCH!
...AND STICKS TO A STRICT DIET BASED ON BOILED VEGETABLES.
AND THIS IS WHERE THE TROUBLE BEGINS, SINCE ASTERIX AND OBELIX, AS THE CHIEF'S ESCORT, HAVE PERMISSION TO SHARE HIS TABLE AT MEAL TIMES...
HEY THERE! ANOTHER BOAR!
SNAP!
AND MORE BEER!
SOME OF THE OTHER PATIENTS BEGIN TO CRACK UP...
BOO...BOOHOOHOOO!
AND SERIOUS INCIDENTS ARE ONLY JUST AVERTED.
IF YOU GO TAKING ADVANTAGE OF HIM TO STEAL HIS BONE BECAUSE HE'S SO SMALL I SHALL POKE YOU IN THE LIVER WITH MY FINGER!
GRRRR!
THE TREATMENT INCLUDES BATHING IN WATER FROM THE HOT SPRINGS.
HEY, ASTERIX, I'D LIKE TO TAKE A DIVE!
HMPFF!
IS IT NICE?
OBELIX, NOOOO!
SPLOSH!

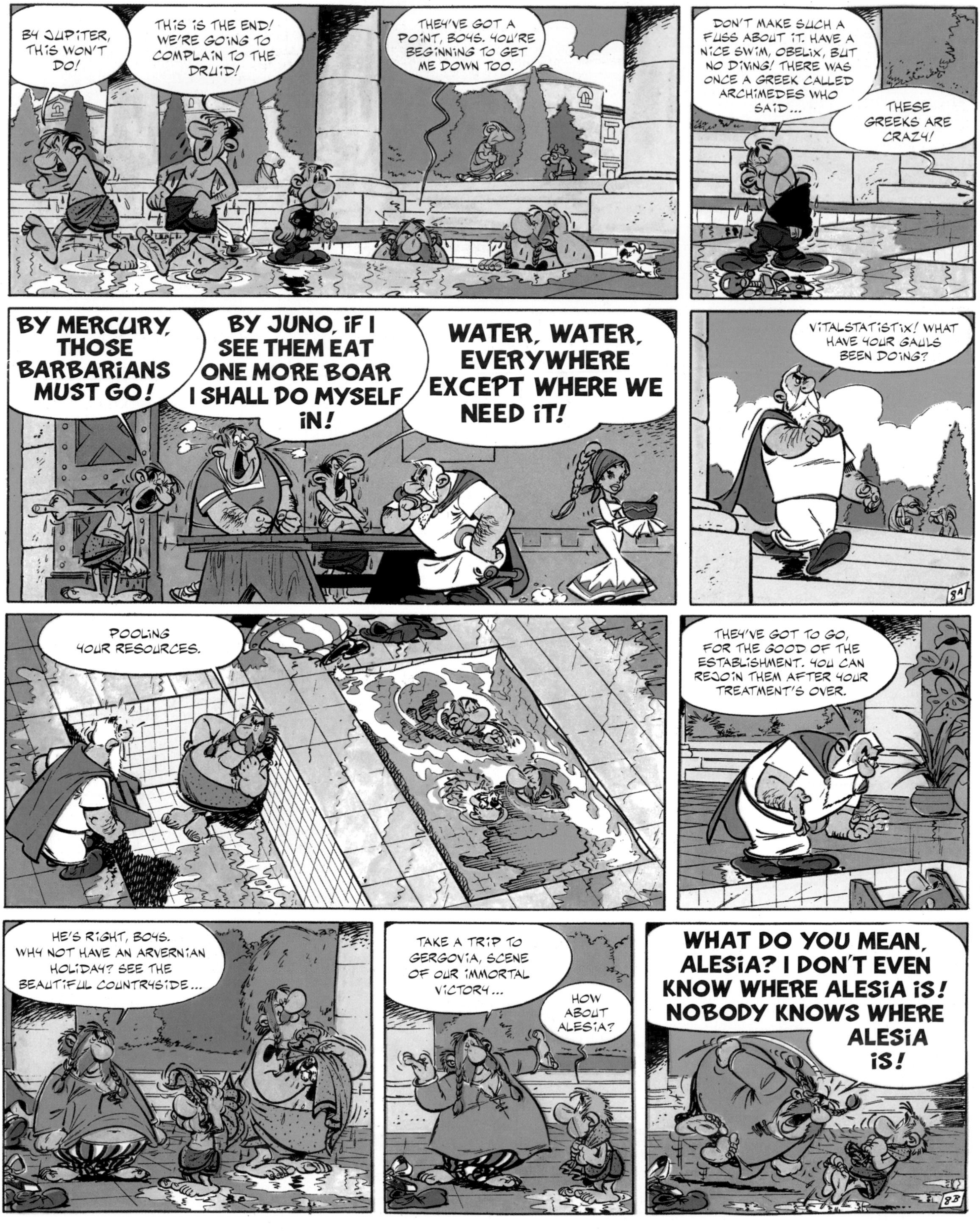
BY JUPITER, THIS WON'T DO!
THIS IS THE END! WE'RE GOING TO COMPLAIN TO THE DRUID!
THEY'VE GOT A POINT, BOYS. YOU'RE BEGINNING TO GET ME DOWN TOO.
DON'T MAKE SUCH A FUSS ABOUT IT. HAVE A NICE SWIM, OBELIX, BUT NO DIVING! THERE WAS ONCE A GREEK CALLED ARCHIMEDES WHO SAID...
THESE GREEKS ARE CRAZY!
BY MERCURY, THOSE BARBARIANS MUST GO!
BY JUNO, IF I SEE THEM EAT ONE MORE BOAR I SHALL DO MYSELF IN!
WATER, WATER, EVERYWHERE EXCEPT WHERE WE NEED IT!
VITALSTATISTIX! WHAT HAVE YOUR GAULS BEEN DOING?
8A
POOLING YOUR RESOURCES.
THEY'VE GOT TO GO, FOR THE GOOD OF THE ESTABLISHMENT. YOU CAN REJOIN THEM AFTER YOUR TREATMENT'S OVER.
HE'S RIGHT, BOYS. WHY NOT HAVE AN ARVERNIAN HOLIDAY? SEE THE BEAUTIFUL COUNTRYSIDE...
TAKE A TRIP TO GERGOVIA, SCENE OF OUR IMMORTAL VICTORY...
HOW ABOUT ALESIA?
WHAT DO YOU MEAN, ALESIA? I DON'T EVEN KNOW WHERE ALESIA IS! NOBODY KNOWS WHERE ALESIA IS!
8B

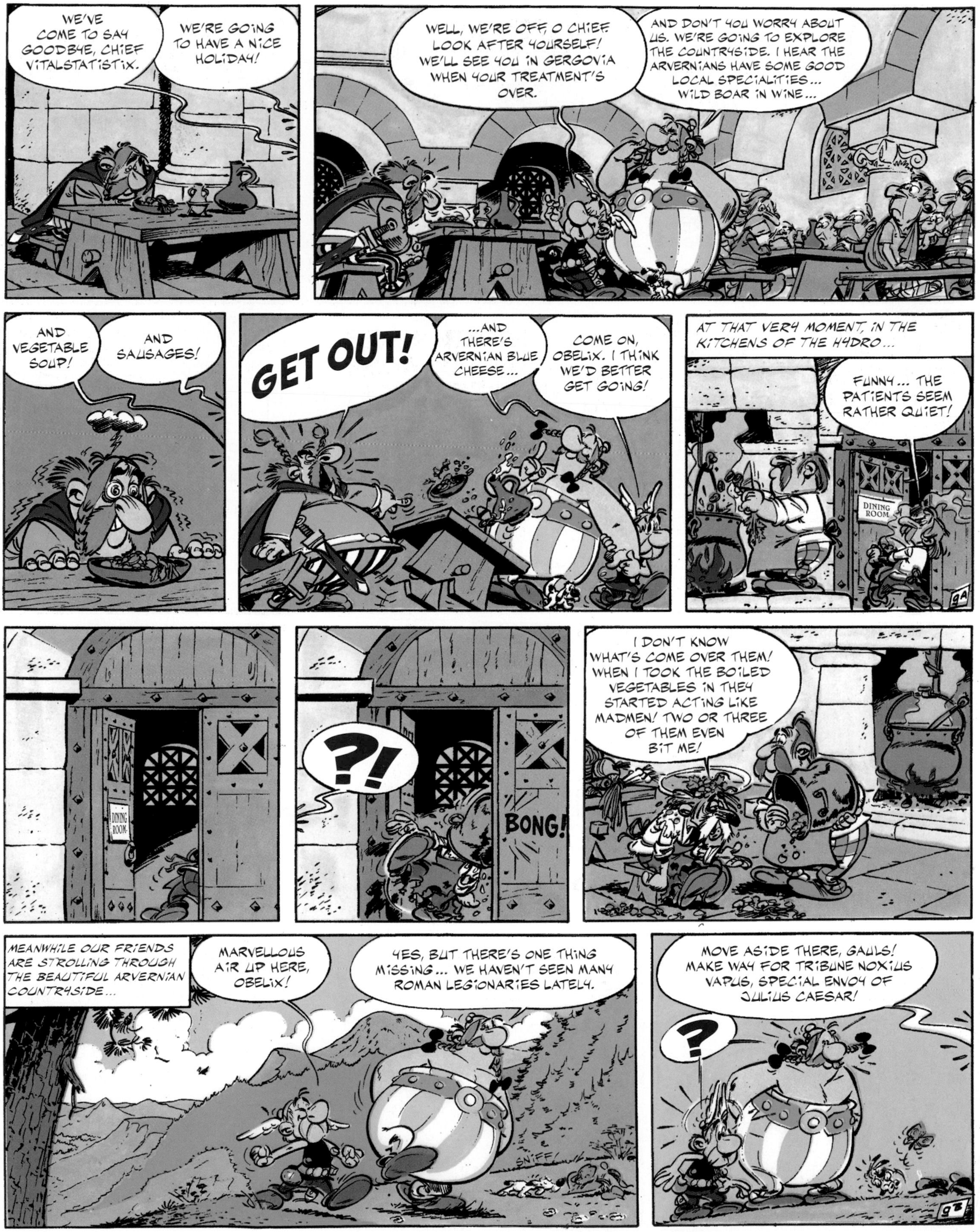
WE'VE COME TO SAY GOODBYE, CHIEF VITALSTATISTIX.
WE'RE GOING TO HAVE A NICE HOLIDAY!
WELL, WE'RE OFF, O CHIEF. LOOK AFTER YOURSELF! WE'LL SEE YOU IN GERGOVIA WHEN YOUR TREATMENT'S OVER.
AND DON'T YOU WORRY ABOUT US. WE'RE GOING TO EXPLORE THE COUNTRYSIDE. I HEAR THE ARVERNIANS HAVE SOME GOOD LOCAL SPECIALITIES... WILD BOAR IN WINE...
AND VEGETABLE SOUP!
AND SAUSAGES!
GET OUT!
...AND THERE'S ARVERNIAN BLUE CHEESE...
COME ON, OBELIX. I THINK WE'D BETTER GET GOING!
AT THAT VERY MOMENT, IN THE KITCHENS OF THE HYDRO...
FUNNY... THE PATIENTS SEEM RATHER QUIET!
DINING ROOM
DINING ROOM
?!
BONG!
I DON'T KNOW WHAT'S COME OVER THEM! WHEN I TOOK THE BOILED VEGETABLES IN THEY STARTED ACTING LIKE MADMEN! TWO OR THREE OF THEM EVEN BIT ME!
MEANWHILE OUR FRIENDS ARE STROLLING THROUGH THE BEAUTIFUL ARVERNIAN COUNTRYSIDE...
MARVELLOUS AIR UP HERE, OBELIX!
YES, BUT THERE'S ONE THING MISSING... WE HAVEN'T SEEN MANY ROMAN LEGIONARIES LATELY.
SNIFF!
MOVE ASIDE THERE, GAULS! MAKE WAY FOR TRIBUNE NOXIUS VAPUS, SPECIAL ENVOY OF JULIUS CAESAR!
?

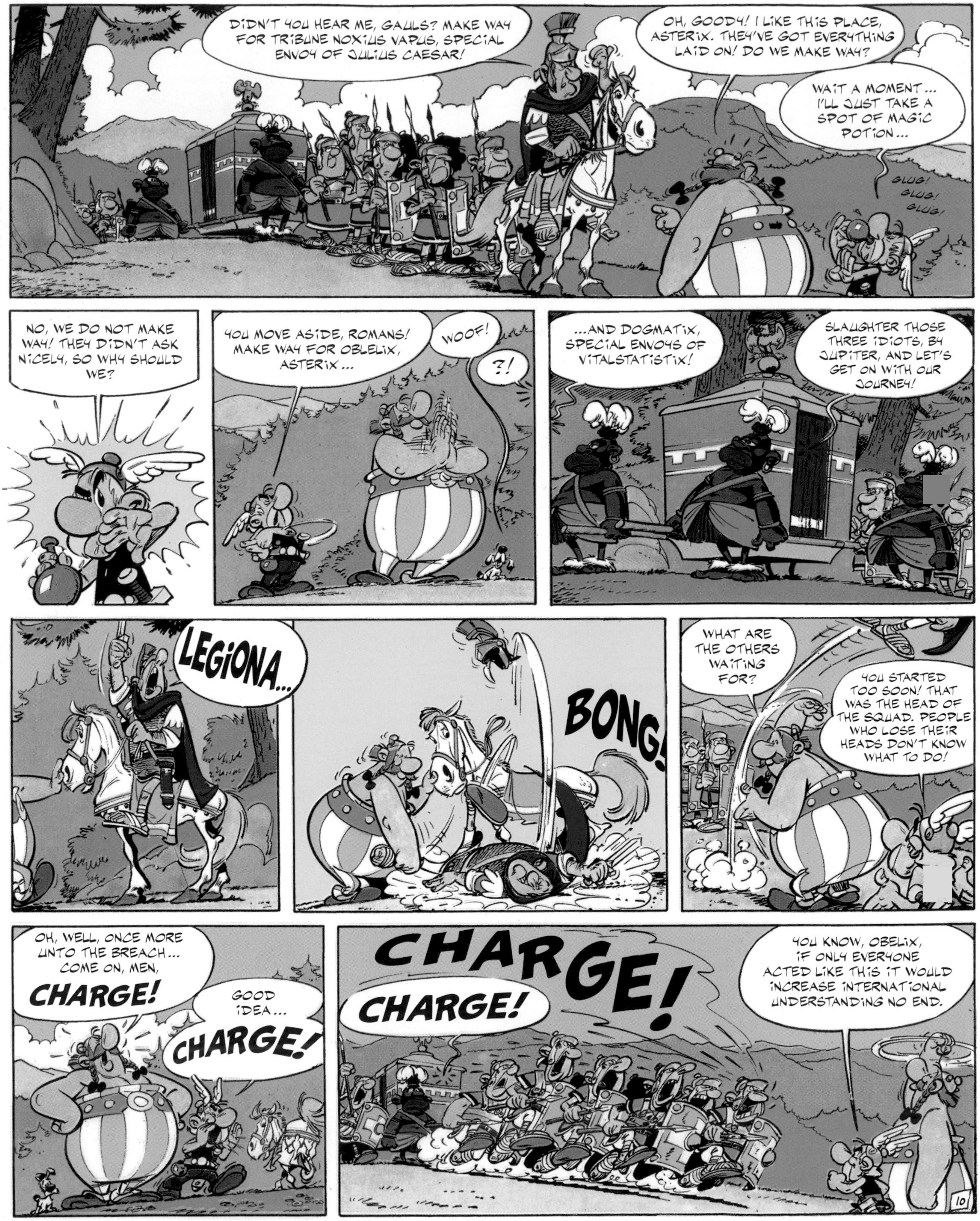
DIDN'T YOU HEAR ME, GAULS? MAKE WAY FOR TRIBUNE NOXIUS VAPUS, SPECIAL ENVOY OF JULIUS CAESAR!
OH, GOODY! I LIKE THIS PLACE, ASTERIX. THEY'VE GOT EVERYTHING LAID ON! DO WE MAKE WAY?
WAIT A MOMENT... I'LL JUST TAKE A SPOT OF MAGIC POTION...
GLUG! GLUG! GLUG!
NO, WE DO NOT MAKE WAY! THEY DIDN'T ASK NICELY, SO WHY SHOULD WE?
YOU MOVE ASIDE, ROMANS! MAKE WAY FOR OBLELIX, ASTERIX...
WOOF!
?!
...AND DOGMATIX, SPECIAL ENVOYS OF VITALSTATISTIX!
SLAUGHTER THOSE THREE IDIOTS, BY JUPITER, AND LET'S GET ON WITH OUR JOURNEY!
LEGIONA...
BONG!
WHAT ARE THE OTHERS WAITING FOR?
YOU STARTED TOO SOON! THAT WAS THE HEAD OF THE SQUAD. PEOPLE WHO LOSE THEIR HEADS DON'T KNOW WHAT TO DO!
OH, WELL, ONCE MORE UNTO THE BREACH... COME ON, MEN, CHARGE!
GOOD IDEA... CHARGE!
CHARGE!
CHARGE!
YOU KNOW, OBELIX, IF ONLY EVERYONE ACTED LIKE THIS IT WOULD INCREASE INTERNATIONAL UNDERSTANDING NO END.
10

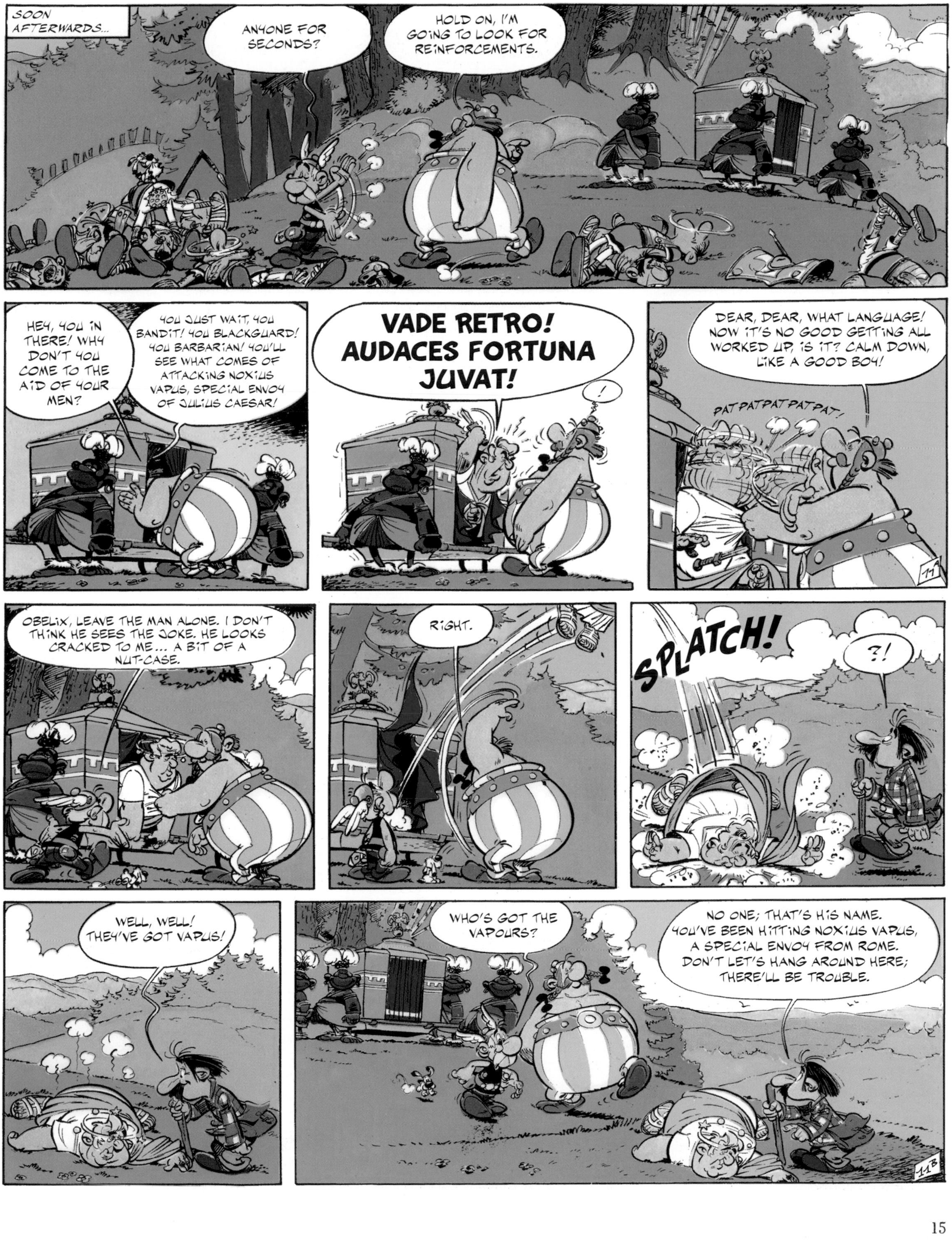

SOON AFTERWARDS...
ANYONE FOR SECONDS?
HOLD ON, I'M GOING TO LOOK FOR REINFORCEMENTS.
HEY, YOU IN THERE! WHY DON'T YOU COME TO THE AID OF YOUR MEN?
YOU JUST WAIT, YOU BANDIT! YOU BLACKGUARD! YOU BARBARIAN! YOU'LL SEE WHAT COMES OF ATTACKING NOXIUS VAPUS, SPECIAL ENVOY OF JULIUS CAESAR!
VADE RETRO! AUDACES FORTUNA JUVAT!
!
DEAR, DEAR, WHAT LANGUAGE! NOW IT'S NO GOOD GETTING ALL WORKED UP, IS IT? CALM DOWN, LIKE A GOOD BOY!
PATPATPATPATPAT!
OBELIX, LEAVE THE MAN ALONE. I DON'T THINK HE SEES THE JOKE. HE LOOKS CRACKED TO ME... A BIT OF A NUT-CASE.
RIGHT.
SPLATCH!
?!
WELL, WELL! THEY'VE GOT VAPUS!
WHO'S GOT THE VAPOURS?
NO ONE; THAT'S HIS NAME. YOU'VE BEEN HITTING NOXIUS VAPUS, A SPECIAL ENVOY FROM ROME. DON'T LET'S HANG AROUND HERE; THERE'LL BE TROUBLE.

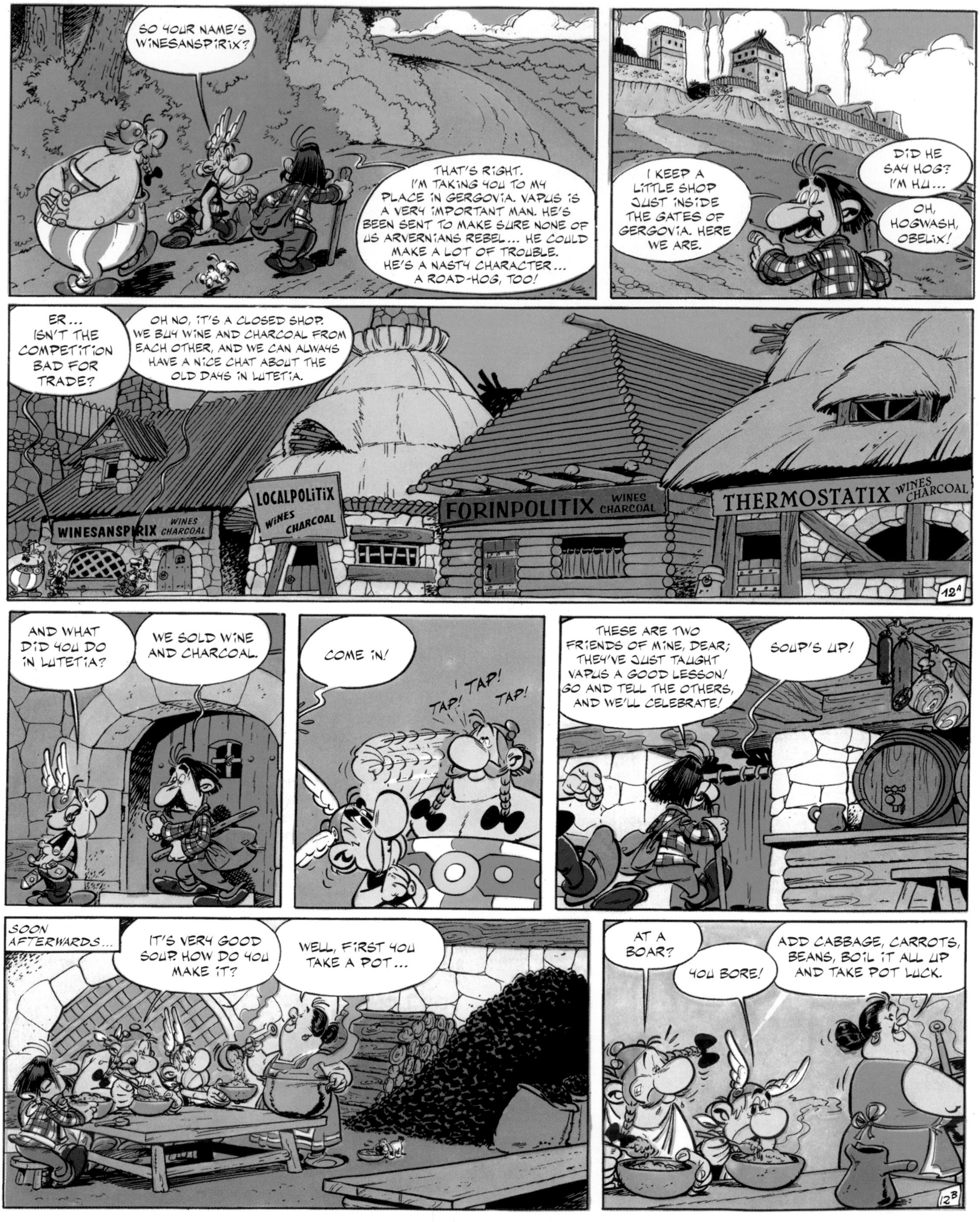
SO YOUR NAME'S WINESANSPIRIX?
THAT'S RIGHT. I'M TAKING YOU TO MY PLACE IN GERGOVIA. VAPUS IS A VERY IMPORTANT MAN. HE'S BEEN SENT TO MAKE SURE NONE OF US ARVERNIANS REBEL... HE COULD MAKE A LOT OF TROUBLE. HE'S A NASTY CHARACTER... A ROAD-HOG, TOO!
I KEEP A LITTLE SHOP JUST INSIDE THE GATES OF GERGOVIA. HERE WE ARE.
DID HE SAY HOG? I'M HU...
OH, HOGWASH, OBELIX!
ER... ISN'T THE COMPETITION BAD FOR TRADE?
OH NO, IT'S A CLOSED SHOP. WE BUY WINE AND CHARCOAL FROM EACH OTHER, AND WE CAN ALWAYS HAVE A NICE CHAT ABOUT THE OLD DAYS IN LUTETIA.
WINESANSPIRIX WINES CHARCOAL
LOCALPOLITIX WINES CHARCOAL
FORINPOLITIX WINES CHARCOAL
THERMOSTATIX WINES CHARCOAL
12A
AND WHAT DID YOU DO IN LUTETIA?
WE SOLD WINE AND CHARCOAL.
COME IN!
TAP! TAP! TAP!
THESE ARE TWO FRIENDS OF MINE, DEAR; THEY'VE JUST TAUGHT VAPUS A GOOD LESSON! GO AND TELL THE OTHERS, AND WE'LL CELEBRATE!
SOUP'S UP!
SOON AFTERWARDS...
IT'S VERY GOOD SOUP. HOW DO YOU MAKE IT?
WELL, FIRST YOU TAKE A POT...
AT A BOAR?
YOU BORE!
ADD CABBAGE, CARROTS, BEANS, BOIL IT ALL UP AND TAKE POT LUCK.
12B

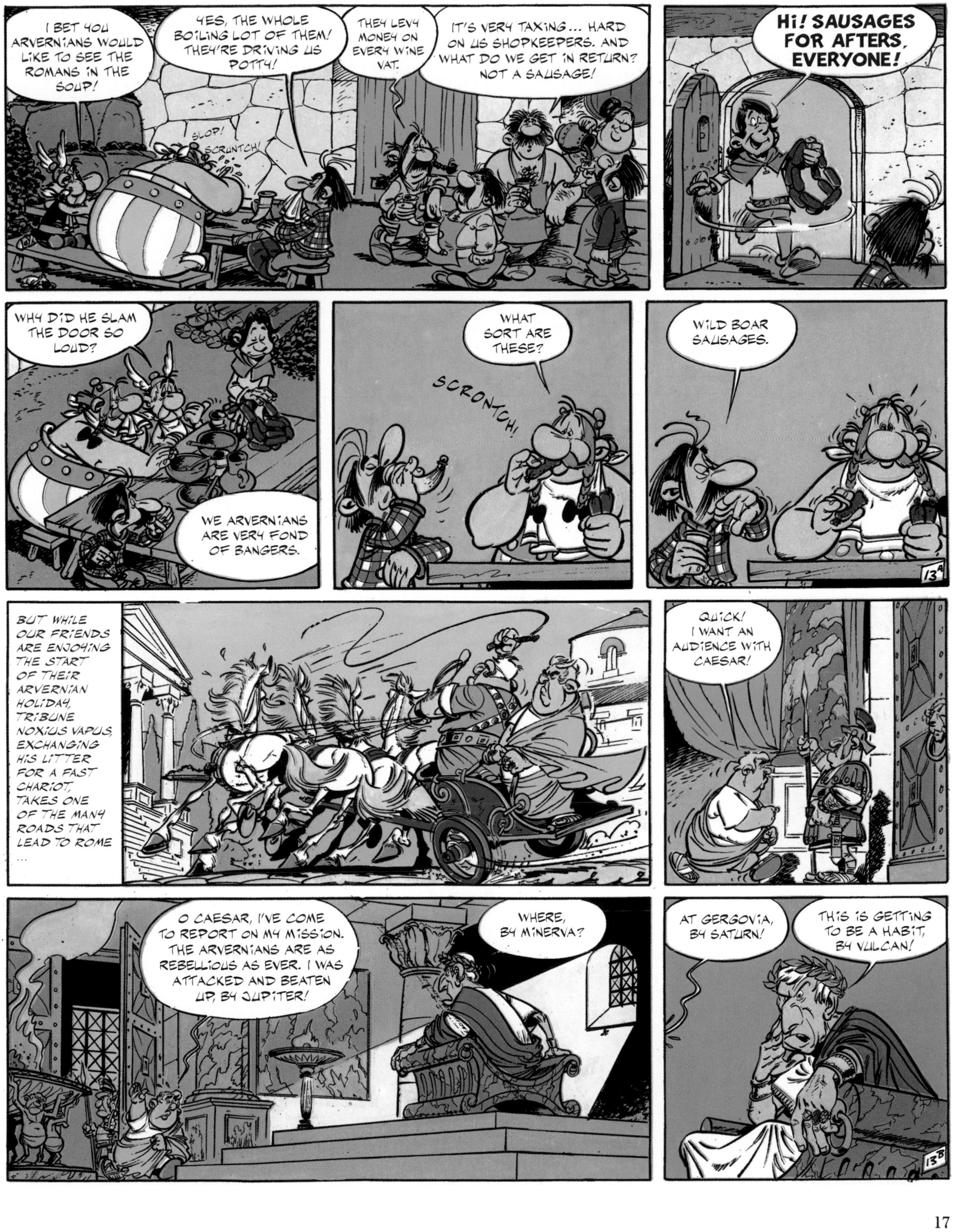
I BET YOU ARVERNIANS WOULD LIKE TO SEE THE ROMANS IN THE SOUP!
YES, THE WHOLE BOILING LOT OF THEM! THEY'RE DRIVING US POTTY!
THEY LEVY MONEY ON EVERY WINE VAT.
IT'S VERY TAXING... HARD ON US SHOPKEEPERS. AND WHAT DO WE GET IN RETURN? NOT A SAUSAGE!
SLOP!
SCRUNTCH!
Hi! SAUSAGES FOR AFTERS, EVERYONE!
WHY DID HE SLAM THE DOOR SO LOUD?
WE ARVERNIANS ARE VERY FOND OF BANGERS.
WHAT SORT ARE THESE?
SCRONTCH!
WILD BOAR SAUSAGES.
13A
BUT WHILE OUR FRIENDS ARE ENJOYING THE START OF THEIR ARVERNIAN HOLIDAY, TRIBUNE NOXIUS VAPUS, EXCHANGING HIS LITTER FOR A FAST CHARIOT, TAKES ONE OF THE MANY ROADS THAT LEAD TO ROME ...
QUICK! I WANT AN AUDIENCE WITH CAESAR!
O CAESAR, I'VE COME TO REPORT ON MY MISSION. THE ARVERNIANS ARE AS REBELLIOUS AS EVER. I WAS ATTACKED AND BEATEN UP, BY JUPITER!
WHERE, BY MINERVA?
AT GERGOVIA, BY SATURN!
THIS IS GETTING TO BE A HABIT, BY VULCAN!
13B

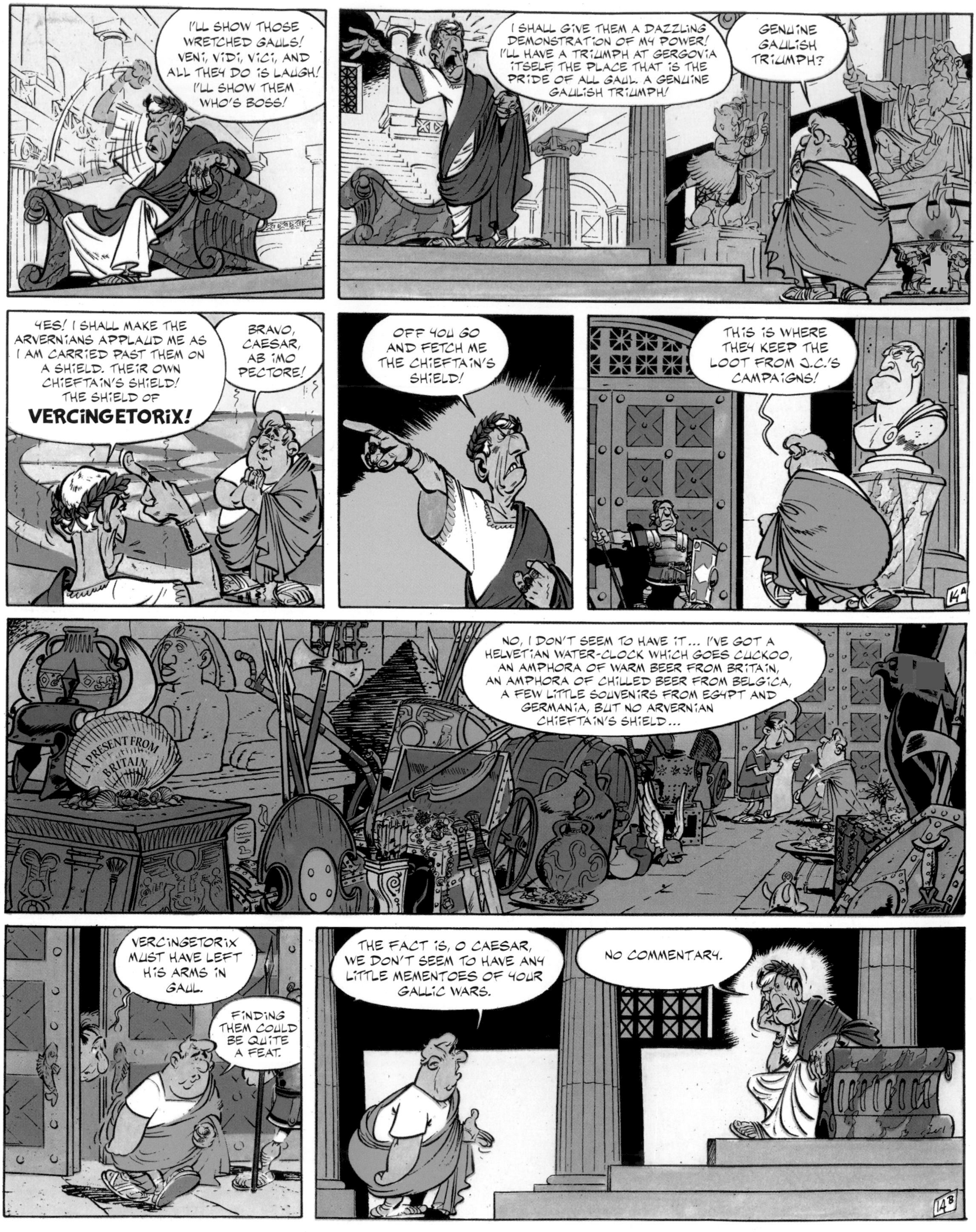
I'LL SHOW THOSE WRETCHED GAULS! VENI, VIDI, VICI, AND ALL THEY DO IS LAUGH! I'LL SHOW THEM WHO'S BOSS!
I SHALL GIVE THEM A DAZZLING DEMONSTRATION OF MY POWER! I'LL HAVE A TRIUMPH AT GERGOVIA ITSELF, THE PLACE THAT IS THE PRIDE OF ALL GAUL. A GENUINE GAULISH TRIUMPH!
GENUINE GAULISH TRIUMPH?
YES! I SHALL MAKE THE ARVERNIANS APPLAUD ME AS I AM CARRIED PAST THEM ON A SHIELD. THEIR OWN CHIEFTAIN'S SHIELD! THE SHIELD OF **VERCINGETORIX!**
BRAVO, CAESAR, AB IMO PECTORE!
OFF YOU GO AND FETCH ME THE CHIEFTAIN'S SHIELD!
THIS IS WHERE THEY KEEP THE LOOT FROM J.C.'S CAMPAIGNS!
14A
NO, I DON'T SEEM TO HAVE IT... I'VE GOT A HELVETIAN WATER-CLOCK WHICH GOES CUCKOO, AN AMPHORA OF WARM BEER FROM BRITAIN, AN AMPHORA OF CHILLED BEER FROM BELGICA, A FEW LITTLE SOUVENIRS FROM EGYPT AND GERMANIA, BUT NO ARVERNIAN CHIEFTAIN'S SHIELD...
A PRESENT FROM BRITAIN
VERCINGETORIX MUST HAVE LEFT HIS ARMS IN GAUL.
FINDING THEM COULD BE QUITE A FEAT.
THE FACT IS, O CAESAR, WE DON'T SEEM TO HAVE ANY LITTLE MEMENTOES OF YOUR GALLIC WARS.
NO COMMENTARY.
14B

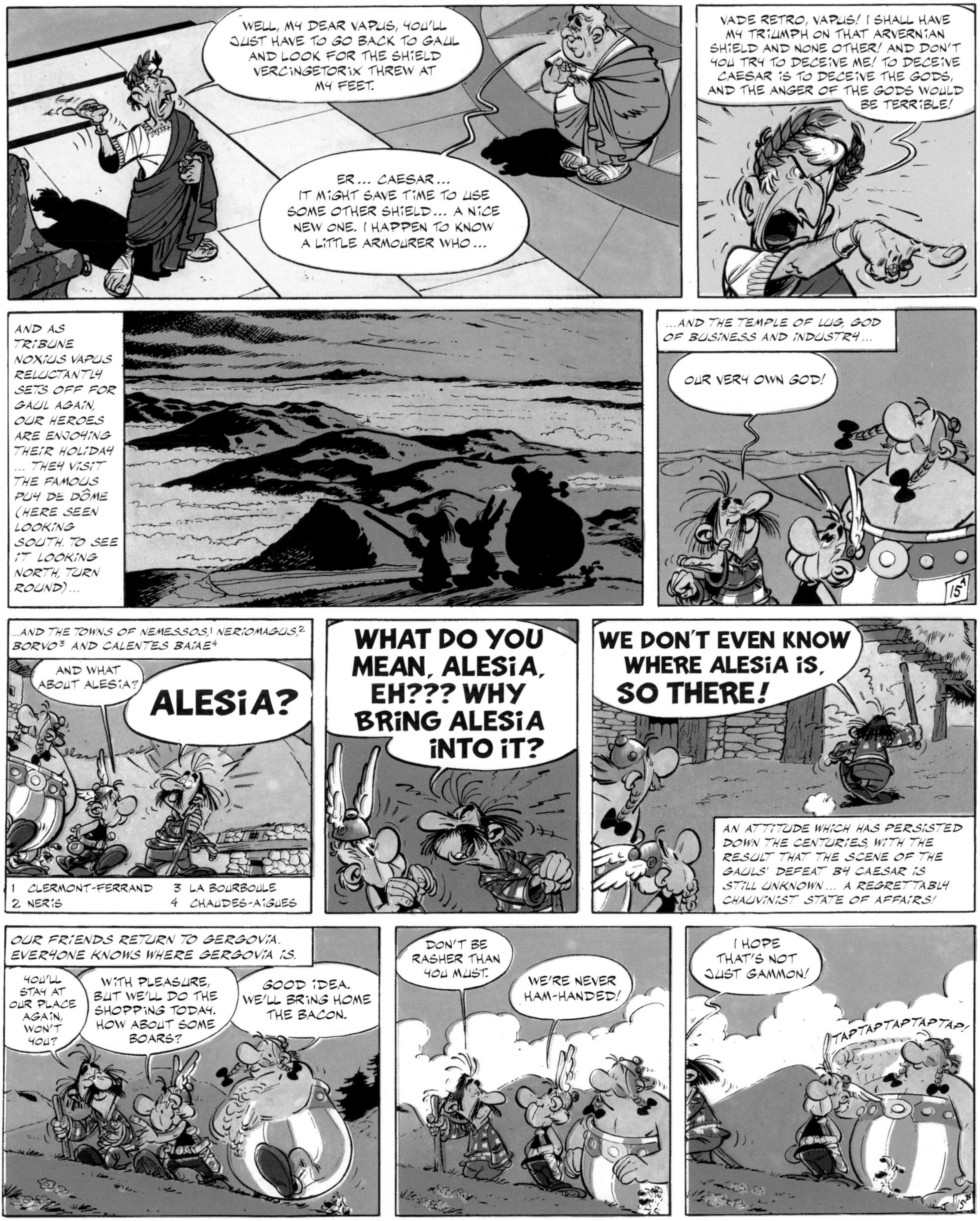

WELL, MY DEAR VAPUS, YOU'LL JUST HAVE TO GO BACK TO GAUL AND LOOK FOR THE SHIELD VERCINGETORIX THREW AT MY FEET.
ER... CAESAR... IT MIGHT SAVE TIME TO USE SOME OTHER SHIELD... A NICE NEW ONE. I HAPPEN TO KNOW A LITTLE ARMOURER WHO...
VADE RETRO, VAPUS! I SHALL HAVE MY TRIUMPH ON THAT ARVERNIAN SHIELD AND NONE OTHER! AND DON'T YOU TRY TO DECEIVE ME! TO DECEIVE CAESAR IS TO DECEIVE THE GODS, AND THE ANGER OF THE GODS WOULD BE TERRIBLE!
AND AS TRIBUNE NOXIUS VAPUS RELUCTANTLY SETS OFF FOR GAUL AGAIN, OUR HEROES ARE ENJOYING THEIR HOLIDAY ... THEY VISIT THE FAMOUS PUY DE DÔME (HERE SEEN LOOKING SOUTH. TO SEE IT LOOKING NORTH, TURN ROUND)...
...AND THE TEMPLE OF LUG, GOD OF BUSINESS AND INDUSTRY...
OUR VERY OWN GOD!
...AND THE TOWNS OF NEMESSOS,1 NERIOMAGUS,2 BORVO3 AND CALENTES BAIAE4
AND WHAT ABOUT ALESIA?
ALESIA?
1 CLERMONT-FERRAND 2 NERIS 3 LA BOURBOULE 4 CHAUDES-AIGUES
WHAT DO YOU MEAN, ALESIA, EH??? WHY BRING ALESIA INTO IT?
WE DON'T EVEN KNOW WHERE ALESIA IS, SO THERE!
AN ATTITUDE WHICH HAS PERSISTED DOWN THE CENTURIES, WITH THE RESULT THAT THE SCENE OF THE GAULS' DEFEAT BY CAESAR IS STILL UNKNOWN... A REGRETTABLY CHAUVINIST STATE OF AFFAIRS!
OUR FRIENDS RETURN TO GERGOVIA. EVERYONE KNOWS WHERE GERGOVIA IS.
YOU'LL STAY AT OUR PLACE AGAIN, WON'T YOU?
WITH PLEASURE, BUT WE'LL DO THE SHOPPING TODAY. HOW ABOUT SOME BOARS?
GOOD IDEA. WE'LL BRING HOME THE BACON.
DON'T BE RASHER THAN YOU MUST.
WE'RE NEVER HAM-HANDED!
I HOPE THAT'S NOT JUST GAMMON!
TAPTAPTAPTAPTAPTAP!

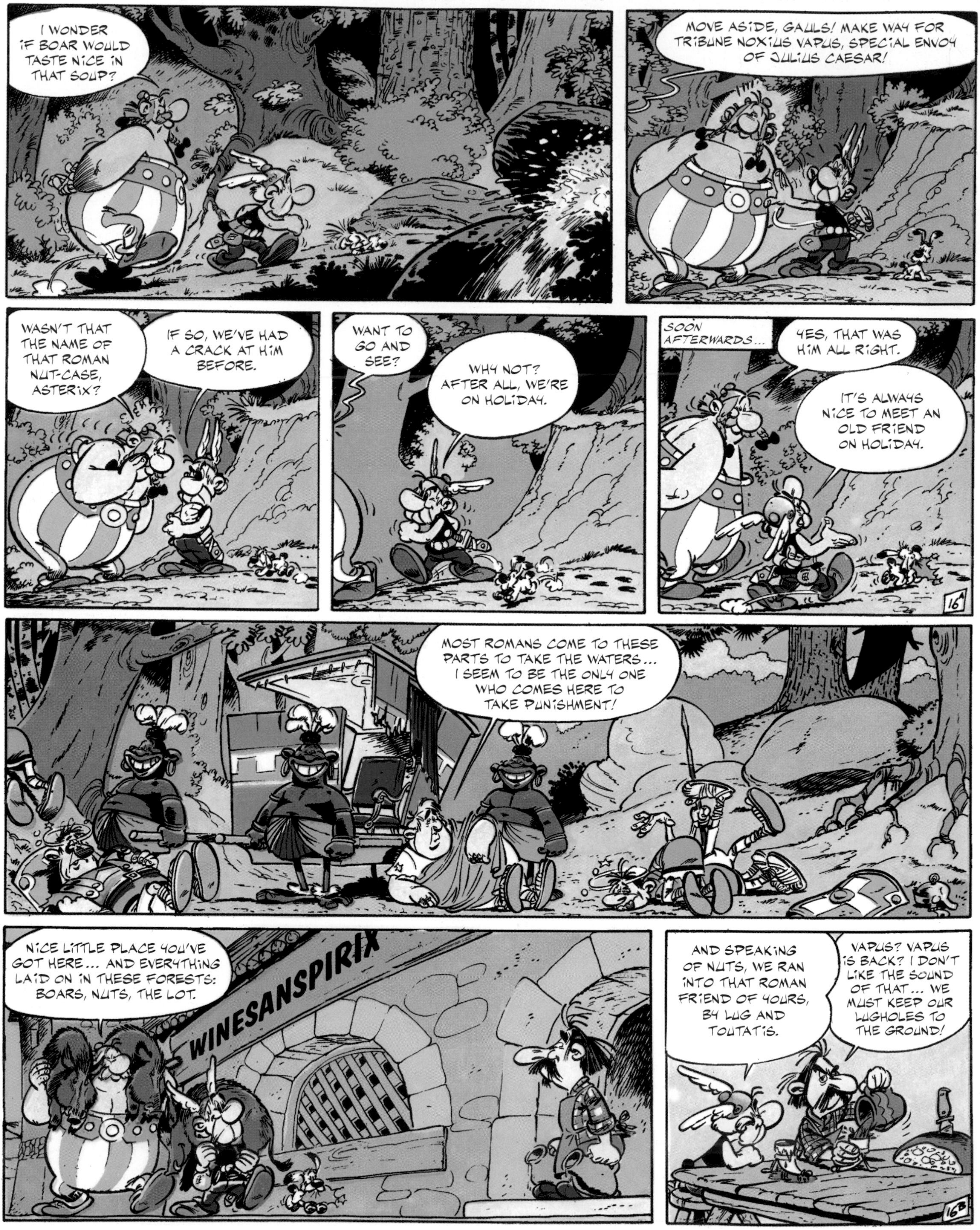
I WONDER IF BOAR WOULD TASTE NICE IN THAT SOUP?
MOVE ASIDE, GAULS! MAKE WAY FOR TRIBUNE NOXIUS VAPUS, SPECIAL ENVOY OF JULIUS CAESAR!
WASN'T THAT THE NAME OF THAT ROMAN NUT-CASE, ASTERIX?
IF SO, WE'VE HAD A CRACK AT HIM BEFORE.
WANT TO GO AND SEE?
WHY NOT? AFTER ALL, WE'RE ON HOLIDAY.
SOON AFTERWARDS...
YES, THAT WAS HIM ALL RIGHT.
IT'S ALWAYS NICE TO MEET AN OLD FRIEND ON HOLIDAY.
16A
MOST ROMANS COME TO THESE PARTS TO TAKE THE WATERS... I SEEM TO BE THE ONLY ONE WHO COMES HERE TO TAKE PUNISHMENT!
NICE LITTLE PLACE YOU'VE GOT HERE... AND EVERYTHING LAID ON IN THESE FORESTS: BOARS, NUTS, THE LOT.
WINESANSPIRIX
AND SPEAKING OF NUTS, WE RAN INTO THAT ROMAN FRIEND OF YOURS, BY LUG AND TOUTATIS.
VAPUS? VAPUS IS BACK? I DON'T LIKE THE SOUND OF THAT... WE MUST KEEP OUR LUGHOLES TO THE GROUND!
16B

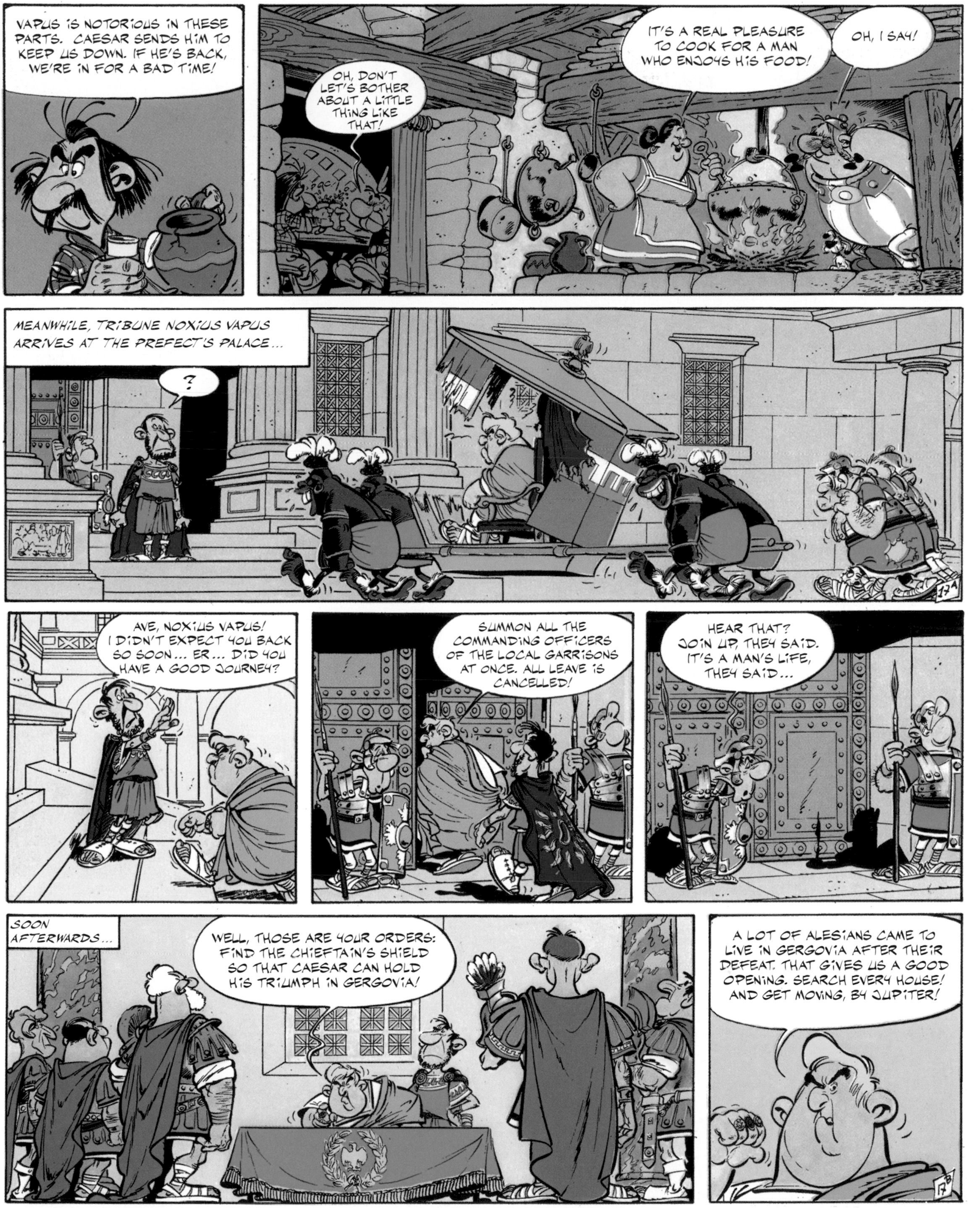
VAPUS IS NOTORIOUS IN THESE PARTS. CAESAR SENDS HIM TO KEEP US DOWN. IF HE'S BACK, WE'RE IN FOR A BAD TIME!
OH, DON'T LET'S BOTHER ABOUT A LITTLE THING LIKE THAT!
IT'S A REAL PLEASURE TO COOK FOR A MAN WHO ENJOYS HIS FOOD!
OH, I SAY!
MEANWHILE, TRIBUNE NOXIUS VAPUS ARRIVES AT THE PREFECT'S PALACE...
?
AVE, NOXIUS VAPUS! I DIDN'T EXPECT YOU BACK SO SOON... ER... DID YOU HAVE A GOOD JOURNEY?
SUMMON ALL THE COMMANDING OFFICERS OF THE LOCAL GARRISONS AT ONCE. ALL LEAVE IS CANCELLED!
HEAR THAT? JOIN UP, THEY SAID. IT'S A MAN'S LIFE, THEY SAID...
SOON AFTERWARDS...
WELL, THOSE ARE YOUR ORDERS: FIND THE CHIEFTAIN'S SHIELD SO THAT CAESAR CAN HOLD HIS TRIUMPH IN GERGOVIA!
A LOT OF ALESIANS CAME TO LIVE IN GERGOVIA AFTER THEIR DEFEAT. THAT GIVES US A GOOD OPENING. SEARCH EVERY HOUSE! AND GET MOVING, BY JUPITER!

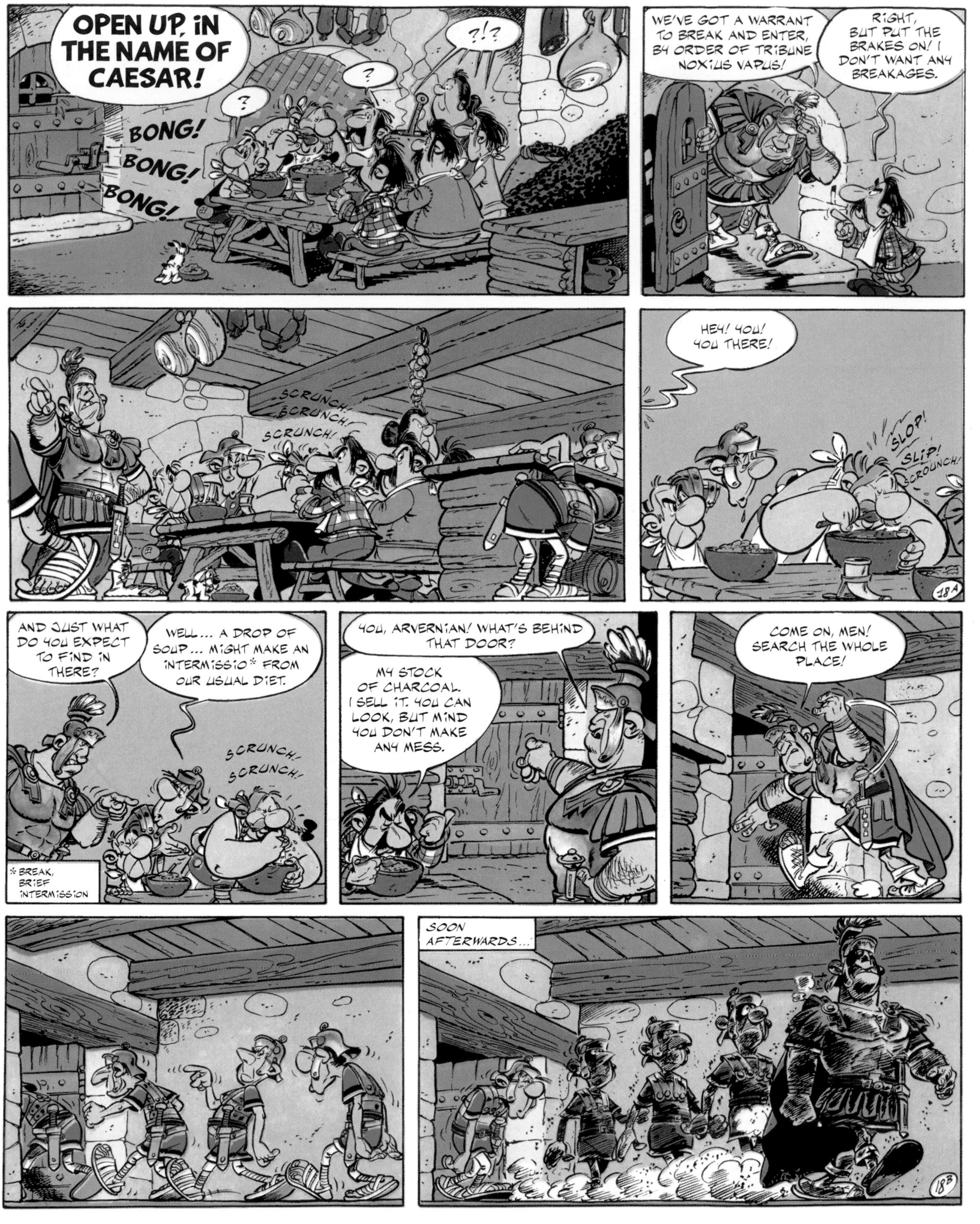
OPEN UP, iN THE NAME OF CAESAR!
?
?
?!?
BONG!
BONG!
BONG!
WE'VE GOT A WARRANT TO BREAK AND ENTER, BY ORDER OF TRIBUNE NOXIUS VAPUS!
RIGHT, BUT PUT THE BRAKES ON! I DON'T WANT ANY BREAKAGES.
SCRUNCH! SCRUNCH!
SCRUNCH!
HEY! YOU! YOU THERE!
SLOP!
SLIP!
SCROUNCH!
AND JUST WHAT DO YOU EXPECT TO FIND IN THERE?
WELL... A DROP OF SOUP... MIGHT MAKE AN INTERMISSIO* FROM OUR USUAL DIET.
SCRUNCH! SCRUNCH!
*BREAK, BRIEF INTERMISSION
YOU, ARVERNIAN! WHAT'S BEHIND THAT DOOR?
MY STOCK OF CHARCOAL. I SELL IT. YOU CAN LOOK, BUT MIND YOU DON'T MAKE ANY MESS.
COME ON, MEN! SEARCH THE WHOLE PLACE!
SOON AFTERWARDS...

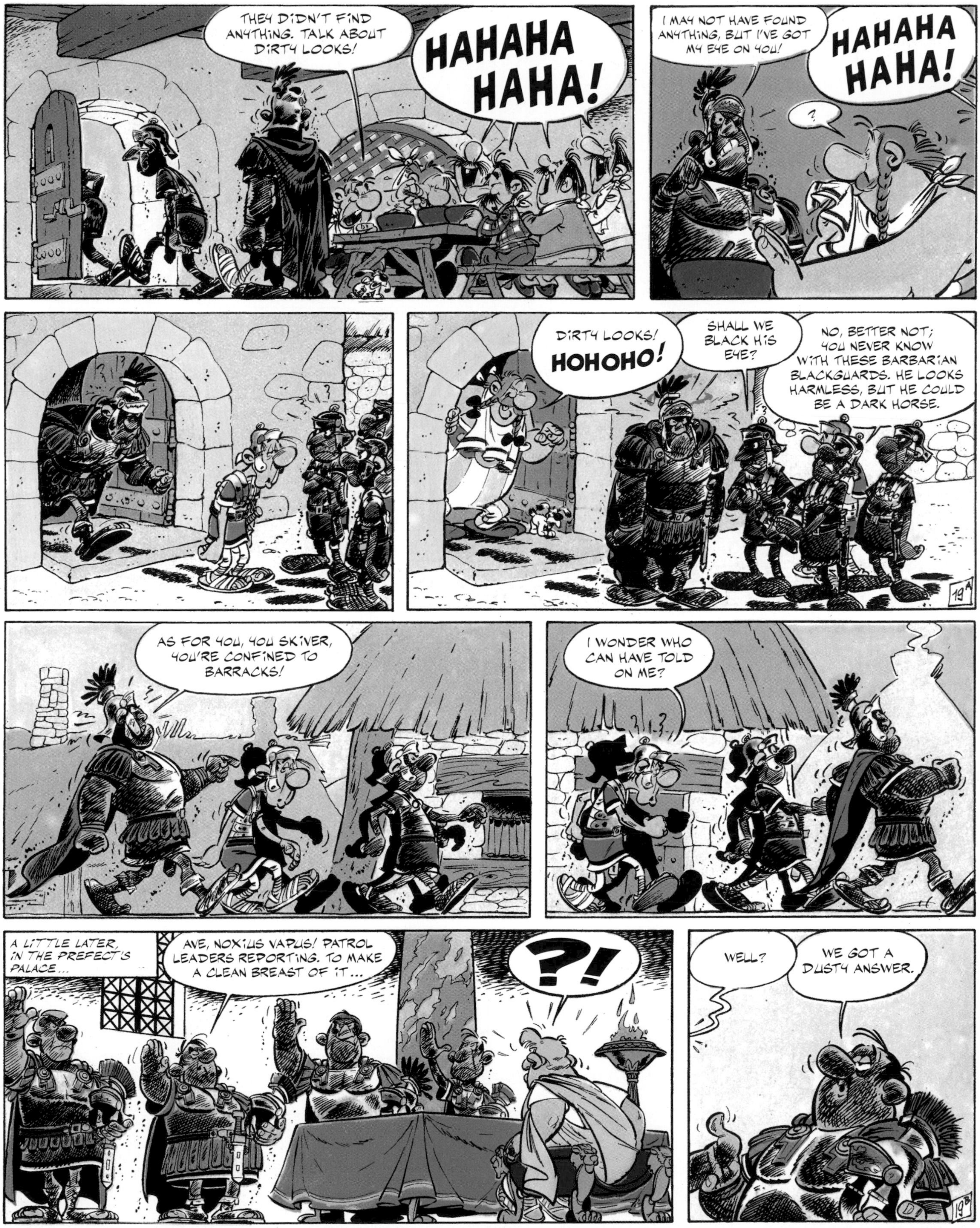
THEY DIDN'T FIND ANYTHING. TALK ABOUT DIRTY LOOKS!
HAHAHA HAHA!
I MAY NOT HAVE FOUND ANYTHING, BUT I'VE GOT MY EYE ON YOU!
HAHAHA HAHA!
?
DIRTY LOOKS! HOHOHO!
SHALL WE BLACK HIS EYE?
NO, BETTER NOT; YOU NEVER KNOW WITH THESE BARBARIAN BLACKGUARDS. HE LOOKS HARMLESS, BUT HE COULD BE A DARK HORSE.
AS FOR YOU, YOU SKIVER, YOU'RE CONFINED TO BARRACKS!
I WONDER WHO CAN HAVE TOLD ON ME?
A LITTLE LATER, IN THE PREFECT'S PALACE...
AVE, NOXIUS VAPUS! PATROL LEADERS REPORTING. TO MAKE A CLEAN BREAST OF IT...
?!
WELL?
WE GOT A DUSTY ANSWER.

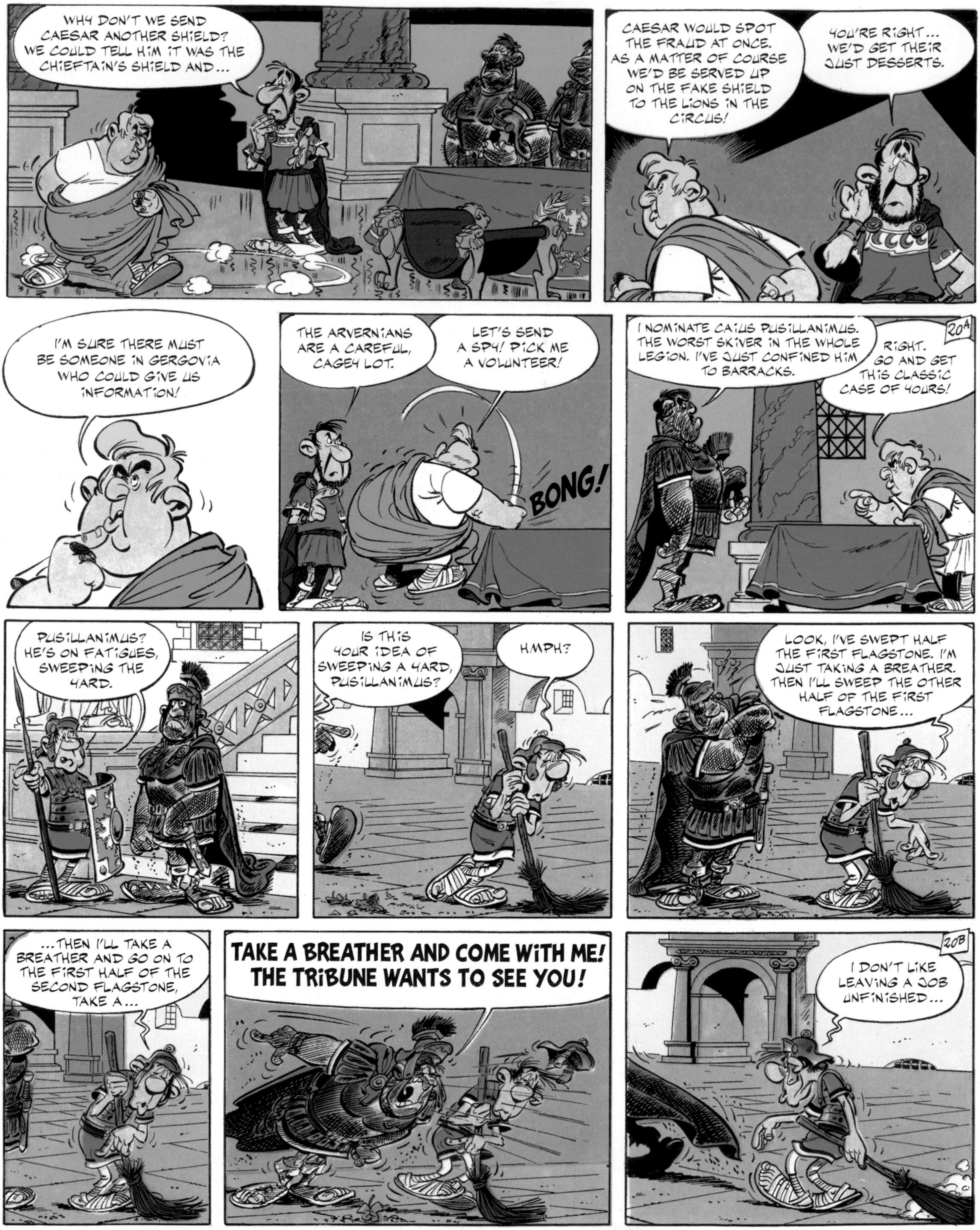

WHY DON'T WE SEND CAESAR ANOTHER SHIELD? WE COULD TELL HIM IT WAS THE CHIEFTAIN'S SHIELD AND...
CAESAR WOULD SPOT THE FRAUD AT ONCE. AS A MATTER OF COURSE WE'D BE SERVED UP ON THE FAKE SHIELD TO THE LIONS IN THE CIRCUS!
YOU'RE RIGHT... WE'D GET THEIR JUST DESSERTS.
I'M SURE THERE MUST BE SOMEONE IN GERGOVIA WHO COULD GIVE US INFORMATION!
THE ARVERNIANS ARE A CAREFUL, CAGEY LOT.
LET'S SEND A SPY! PICK ME A VOLUNTEER!
BONG!
20A
I NOMINATE CAIUS PUSILLANIMUS. THE WORST SKIVER IN THE WHOLE LEGION. I'VE JUST CONFINED HIM TO BARRACKS.
RIGHT. GO AND GET THIS CLASSIC CASE OF YOURS!
PUSILLANIMUS? HE'S ON FATIGUES, SWEEPING THE YARD.
IS THIS YOUR IDEA OF SWEEPING A YARD, PUSILLANIMUS?
HMPH?
LOOK, I'VE SWEPT HALF THE FIRST FLAGSTONE. I'M JUST TAKING A BREATHER. THEN I'LL SWEEP THE OTHER HALF OF THE FIRST FLAGSTONE...
...THEN I'LL TAKE A BREATHER AND GO ON TO THE FIRST HALF OF THE SECOND FLAGSTONE, TAKE A...
TAKE A BREATHER AND COME WITH ME! THE TRIBUNE WANTS TO SEE YOU!
20B
I DON'T LIKE LEAVING A JOB UNFINISHED...

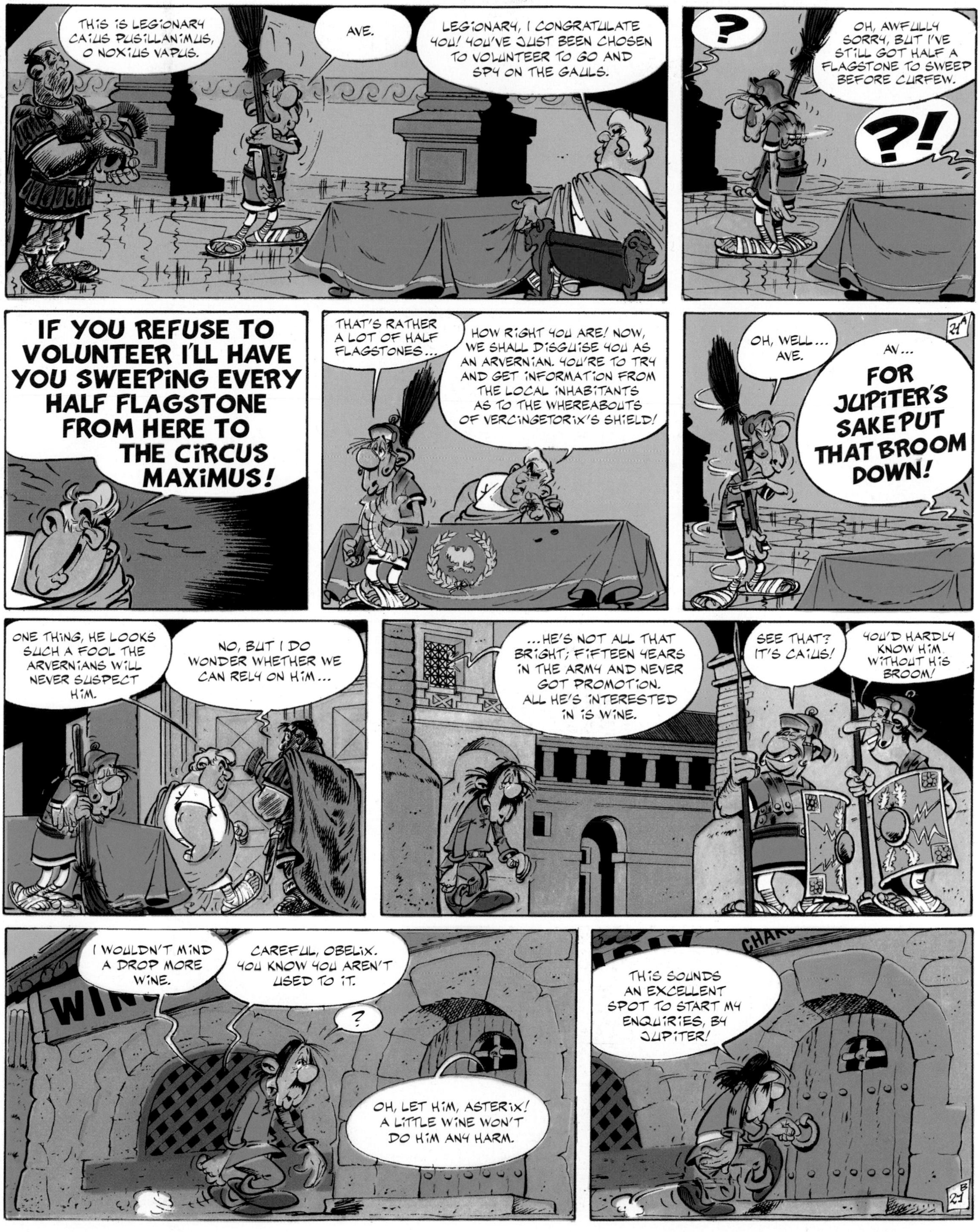

THIS IS LEGIONARY CAIUS PUSILLANIMUS, O NOXIUS VAPUS.
AVE.
LEGIONARY, I CONGRATULATE YOU! YOU'VE JUST BEEN CHOSEN TO VOLUNTEER TO GO AND SPY ON THE GAULS.
?
OH, AWFULLY SORRY, BUT I'VE STILL GOT HALF A FLAGSTONE TO SWEEP BEFORE CURFEW.
?!
IF YOU REFUSE TO VOLUNTEER I'LL HAVE YOU SWEEPING EVERY HALF FLAGSTONE FROM HERE TO THE CIRCUS MAXIMUS!
THAT'S RATHER A LOT OF HALF FLAGSTONES...
HOW RIGHT YOU ARE! NOW, WE SHALL DISGUISE YOU AS AN ARVERNIAN. YOU'RE TO TRY AND GET INFORMATION FROM THE LOCAL INHABITANTS AS TO THE WHEREABOUTS OF VERCINGETORIX'S SHIELD!
OH, WELL... AVE.
AV... FOR JUPITER'S SAKE PUT THAT BROOM DOWN!
ONE THING, HE LOOKS SUCH A FOOL THE ARVERNIANS WILL NEVER SUSPECT HIM.
NO, BUT I DO WONDER WHETHER WE CAN RELY ON HIM...
...HE'S NOT ALL THAT BRIGHT; FIFTEEN YEARS IN THE ARMY AND NEVER GOT PROMOTION. ALL HE'S INTERESTED IN IS WINE.
SEE THAT? IT'S CAIUS!
YOU'D HARDLY KNOW HIM WITHOUT HIS BROOM!
I WOULDN'T MIND A DROP MORE WINE.
CAREFUL, OBELIX. YOU KNOW YOU AREN'T USED TO IT.
?
OH, LET HIM, ASTERIX! A LITTLE WINE WON'T DO HIM ANY HARM.
THIS SOUNDS AN EXCELLENT SPOT TO START MY ENQUIRIES, BY JUPITER!

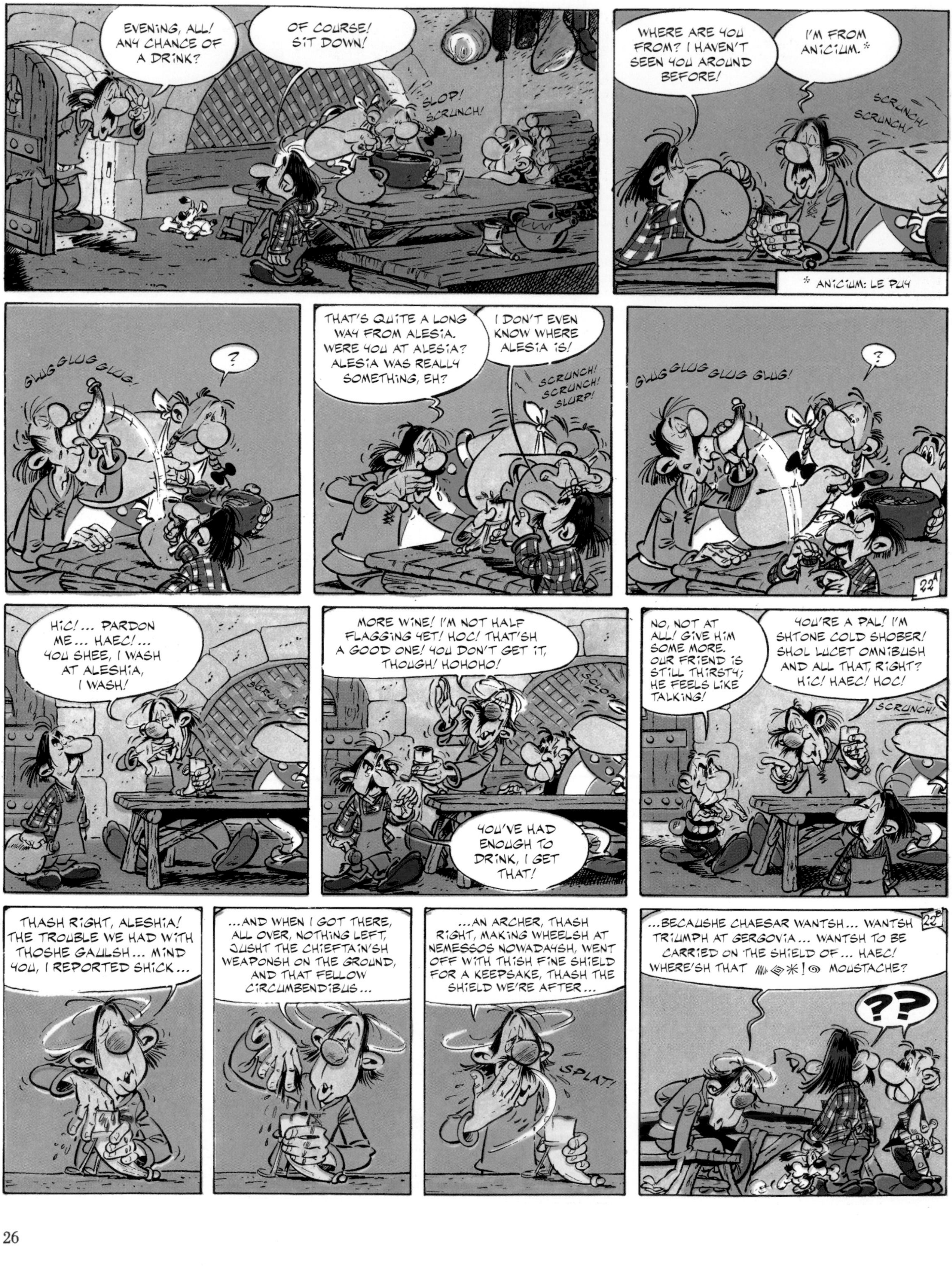
EVENING, ALL! ANY CHANCE OF A DRINK?
OF COURSE! SIT DOWN!
SLOP! SCRUNCH!
WHERE ARE YOU FROM? I HAVEN'T SEEN YOU AROUND BEFORE!
I'M FROM ANICIUM.*
SCRUNCH! SCRUNCH!
* ANICIUM: LE PUY
GLUG GLUG GLUG!
?
THAT'S QUITE A LONG WAY FROM ALESIA. WERE YOU AT ALESIA? ALESIA WAS REALLY SOMETHING, EH?
I DON'T EVEN KNOW WHERE ALESIA IS!
SCRUNCH! SCRUNCH! SLURP!
GLUG GLUG GLUG GLUG!
?
HIC! ... PARDON ME ... HAEC! ... YOU SHEE, I WASH AT ALESHIA, I WASH!
SCRUNCH
MORE WINE! I'M NOT HALF FLAGGING YET! HOC! THAT'SH A GOOD ONE! YOU DON'T GET IT, THOUGH! HOHOHO!
SCLOP
YOU'VE HAD ENOUGH TO DRINK, I GET THAT!
NO, NOT AT ALL! GIVE HIM SOME MORE. OUR FRIEND IS STILL THIRSTY; HE FEELS LIKE TALKING!
YOU'RE A PAL! I'M SHTONE COLD SHOBER! SHOL LUCET OMNIBUSH AND ALL THAT, RIGHT? HIC! HAEC! HOC!
SCRUNCH!
THASH RIGHT, ALESHIA! THE TROUBLE WE HAD WITH THOSHE GAULSH ... MIND YOU, I REPORTED SHICK ...
... AND WHEN I GOT THERE, ALL OVER, NOTHING LEFT, JUSHT THE CHIEFTAIN'SH WEAPONSH ON THE GROUND, AND THAT FELLOW CIRCUMBENDIBUS ...
... AN ARCHER, THASH RIGHT, MAKING WHEELSH AT NEMESSOS NOWADAYSH, WENT OFF WITH THISH FINE SHIELD FOR A KEEPSAKE, THASH THE SHIELD WE'RE AFTER ...
SPLAT!
... BECAUSHE CHAESAR WANTSH ... WANTSH TRIUMPH AT GERGOVIA ... WANTSH TO BE CARRIED ON THE SHIELD OF ... HAEC! WHERE'SH THAT ✱! MOUSTACHE?
??

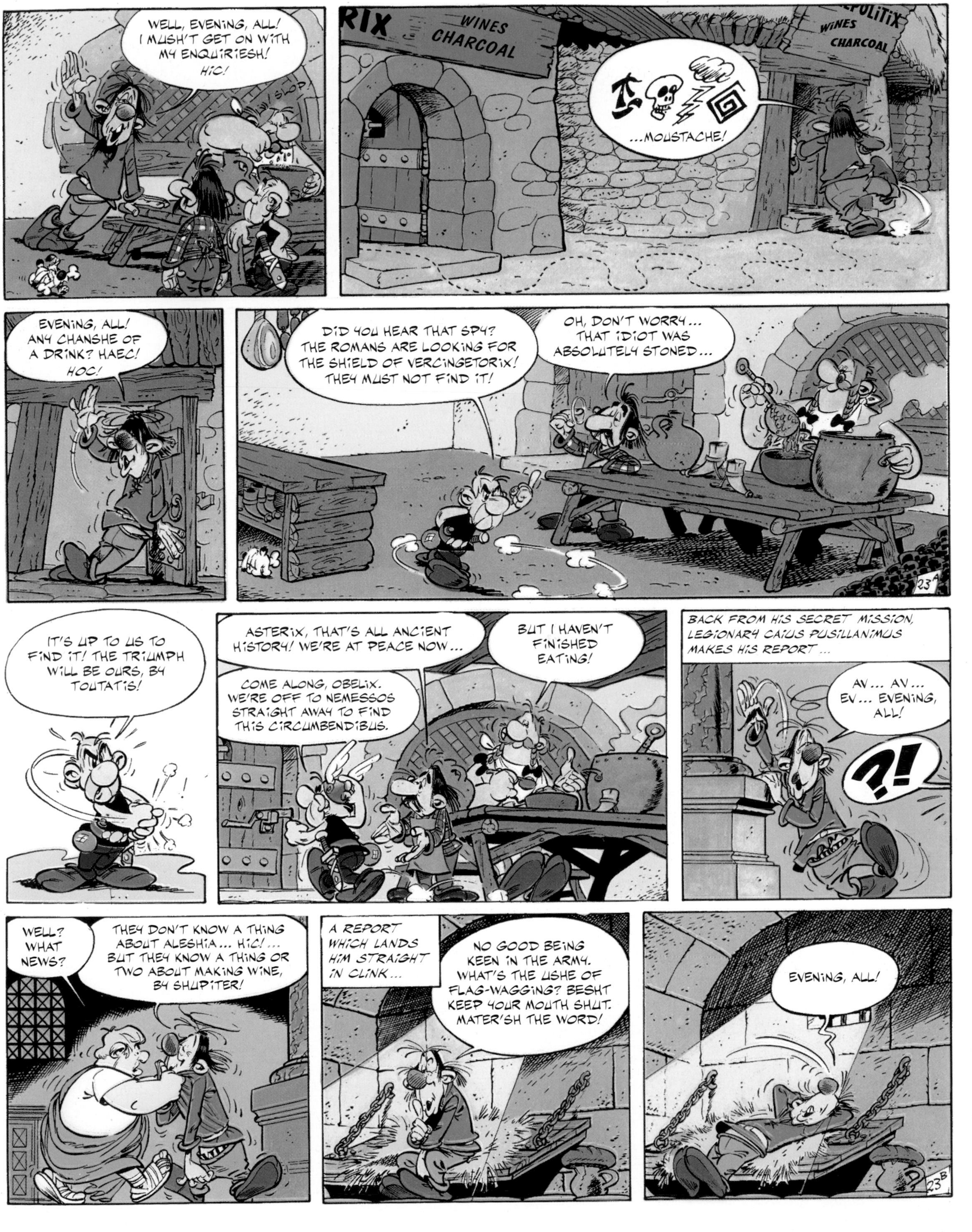
WELL, EVENING, ALL! I MUSH'T GET ON WITH MY ENQUIRIESH! HIC!
SLOP
WINES CHARCOAL
...MOUSTACHE!
EVENING, ALL! ANY CHANSHE OF A DRINK? HAEC! HOC!
DID YOU HEAR THAT SPY? THE ROMANS ARE LOOKING FOR THE SHIELD OF VERCINGETORIX! THEY MUST NOT FIND IT!
OH, DON'T WORRY... THAT IDIOT WAS ABSOLUTELY STONED...
IT'S UP TO US TO FIND IT! THE TRIUMPH WILL BE OURS, BY TOUTATIS!
ASTERIX, THAT'S ALL ANCIENT HISTORY! WE'RE AT PEACE NOW...
BUT I HAVEN'T FINISHED EATING!
COME ALONG, OBELIX. WE'RE OFF TO NEMESSOS STRAIGHT AWAY TO FIND THIS CIRCUMBENDIBUS.
BACK FROM HIS SECRET MISSION, LEGIONARY CAIUS PUSILLANIMUS MAKES HIS REPORT...
AV... AV... EV... EVENING, ALL!
?!
WELL? WHAT NEWS?
THEY DON'T KNOW A THING ABOUT ALESHIA... HIC!... BUT THEY KNOW A THING OR TWO ABOUT MAKING WINE, BY SHUPITER!
A REPORT WHICH LANDS HIM STRAIGHT IN CLINK...
NO GOOD BEING KEEN IN THE ARMY. WHAT'S THE USHE OF FLAG-WAGGING? BESHT KEEP YOUR MOUTH SHUT. MATER'SH THE WORD!
EVENING, ALL!

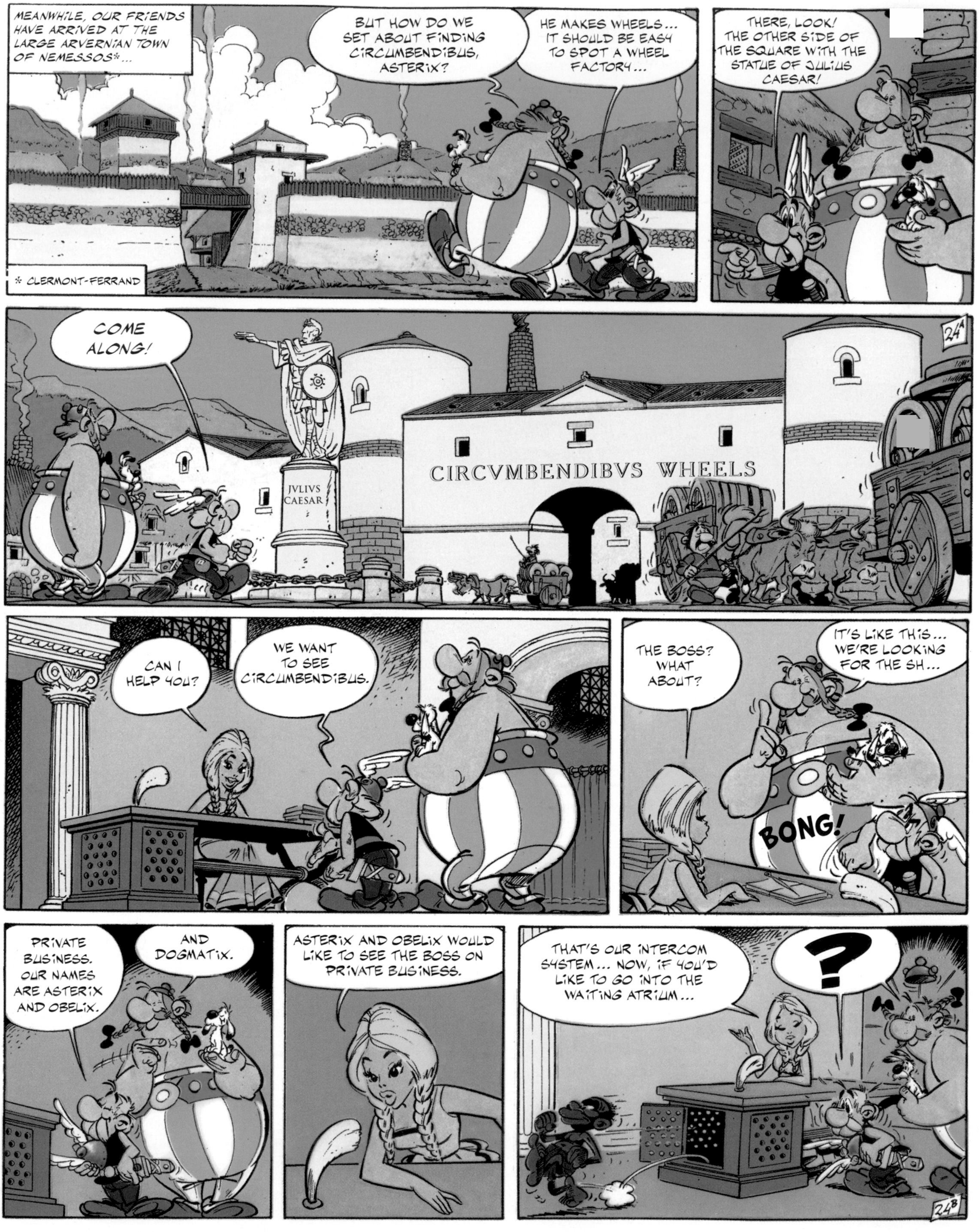

MEANWHILE, OUR FRIENDS HAVE ARRIVED AT THE LARGE ARVERNIAN TOWN OF NEMESSOS*...
* CLERMONT-FERRAND
BUT HOW DO WE SET ABOUT FINDING CIRCUMBENDIBUS, ASTERIX?
HE MAKES WHEELS... IT SHOULD BE EASY TO SPOT A WHEEL FACTORY...
THERE, LOOK! THE OTHER SIDE OF THE SQUARE WITH THE STATUE OF JULIUS CAESAR!
COME ALONG!
JVLIVS CAESAR
CIRCVMBENDIBVS WHEELS
24A
CAN I HELP YOU?
WE WANT TO SEE CIRCUMBENDIBUS.
THE BOSS? WHAT ABOUT?
IT'S LIKE THIS... WE'RE LOOKING FOR THE SH...
BONG!
PRIVATE BUSINESS. OUR NAMES ARE ASTERIX AND OBELIX.
AND DOGMATIX.
ASTERIX AND OBELIX WOULD LIKE TO SEE THE BOSS ON PRIVATE BUSINESS.
THAT'S OUR INTERCOM SYSTEM... NOW, IF YOU'D LIKE TO GO INTO THE WAITING ATRIUM...
?
24B

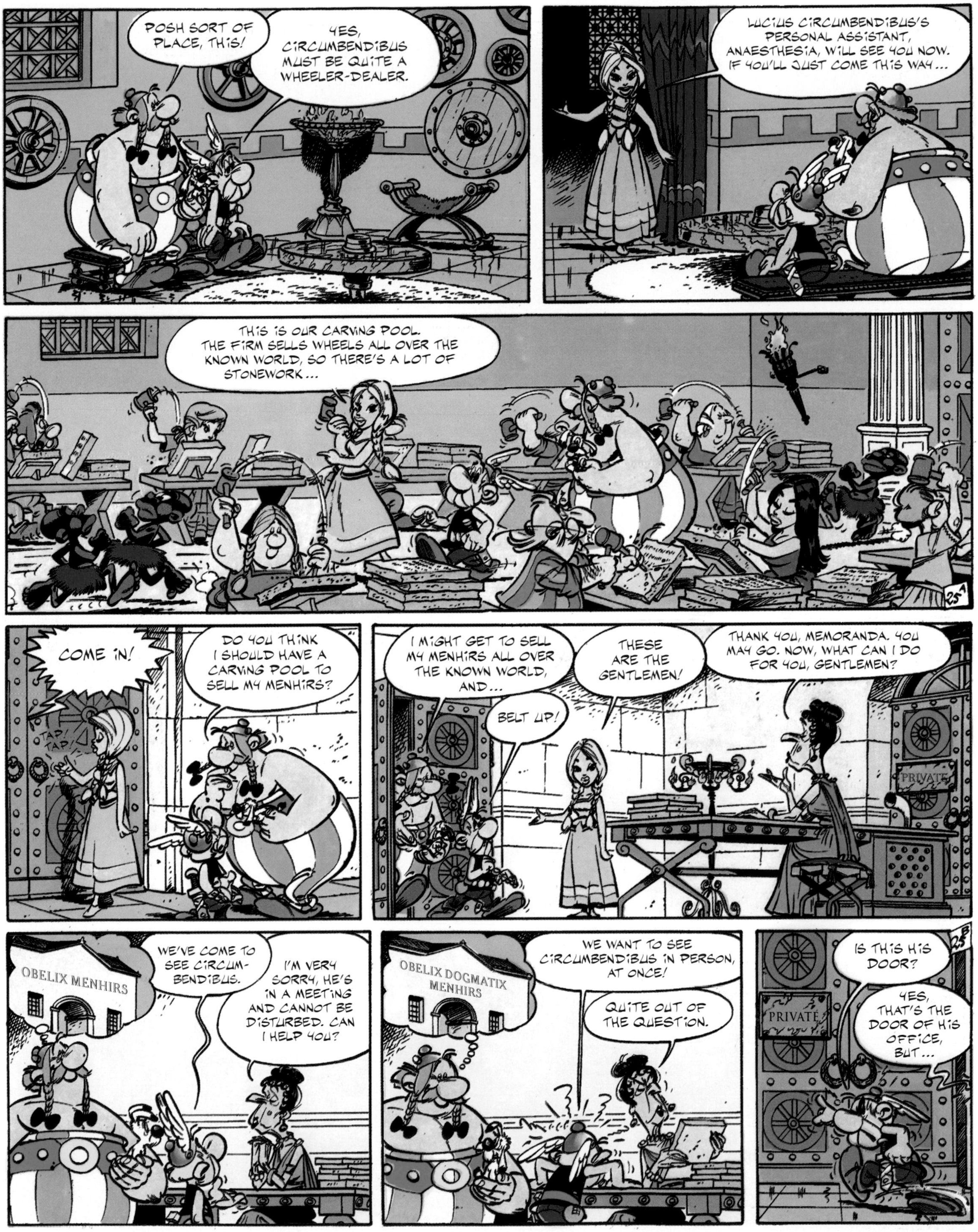

POSH SORT OF PLACE, THIS!
YES, CIRCUMBENDIBUS MUST BE QUITE A WHEELER-DEALER.
LUCIUS CIRCUMBENDIBUS'S PERSONAL ASSISTANT, ANAESTHESIA, WILL SEE YOU NOW. IF YOU'LL JUST COME THIS WAY...
THIS IS OUR CARVING POOL. THE FIRM SELLS WHEELS ALL OVER THE KNOWN WORLD, SO THERE'S A LOT OF STONEWORK...
TAP! TAP!
COME IN!
DO YOU THINK I SHOULD HAVE A CARVING POOL TO SELL MY MENHIRS?
I MIGHT GET TO SELL MY MENHIRS ALL OVER THE KNOWN WORLD, AND...
BELT UP!
THESE ARE THE GENTLEMEN!
THANK YOU, MEMORANDA. YOU MAY GO. NOW, WHAT CAN I DO FOR YOU, GENTLEMEN?
PRIVATE
OBELIX MENHIRS
WE'VE COME TO SEE CIRCUM-BENDIBUS.
I'M VERY SORRY, HE'S IN A MEETING AND CANNOT BE DISTURBED. CAN I HELP YOU?
OBELIX DOGMATIX MENHIRS
WE WANT TO SEE CIRCUMBENDIBUS IN PERSON, AT ONCE!
QUITE OUT OF THE QUESTION.
PRIVATE
IS THIS HIS DOOR?
YES, THAT'S THE DOOR OF HIS OFFICE, BUT...

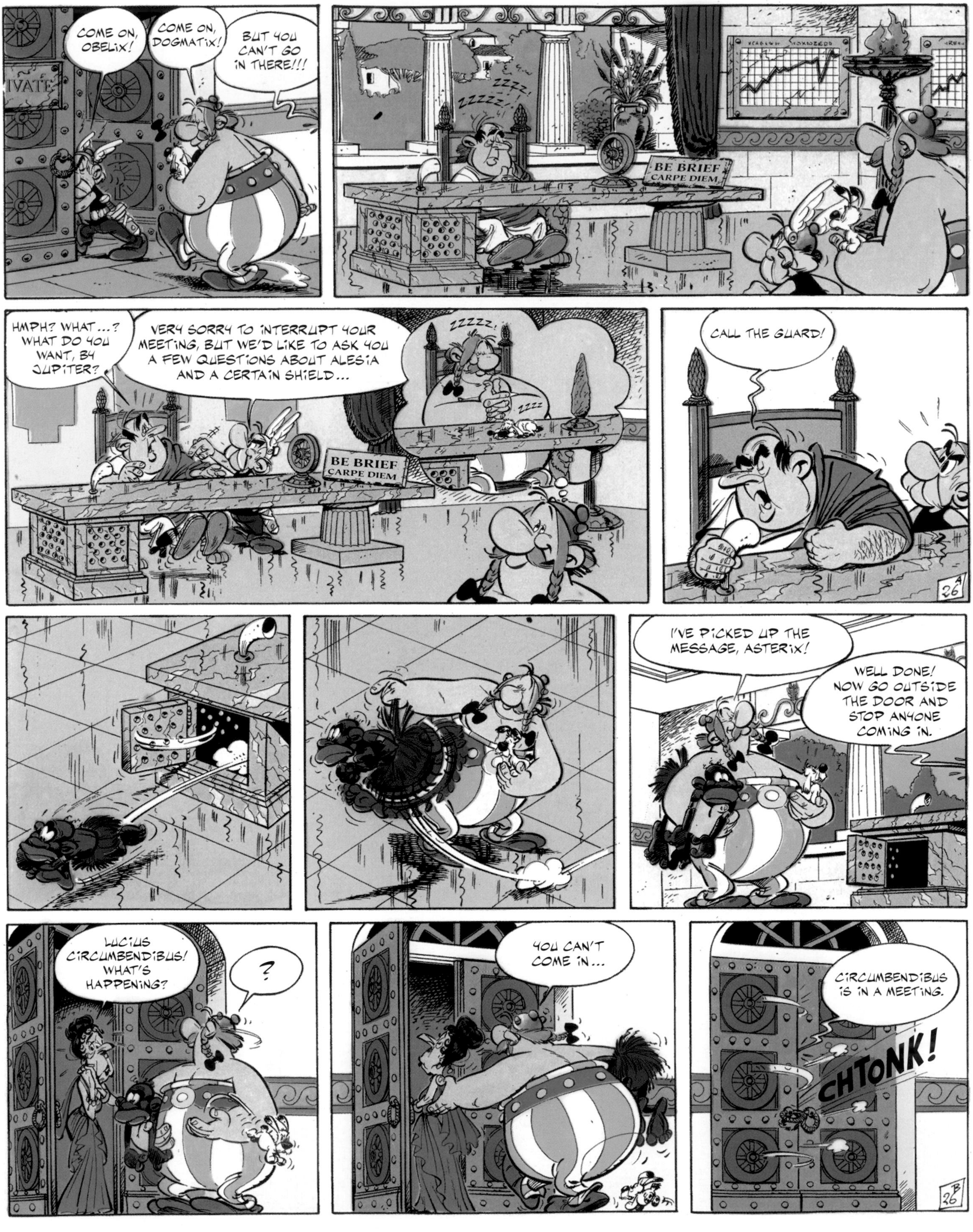
IVATE
COME ON, OBELIX!
COME ON, DOGMATIX!
BUT YOU CAN'T GO IN THERE!!!
ZZZZZ
ZZZZZ
BE BRIEF CARPE DIEM
HMPH? WHAT...? WHAT DO YOU WANT, BY JUPITER?
VERY SORRY TO INTERRUPT YOUR MEETING, BUT WE'D LIKE TO ASK YOU A FEW QUESTIONS ABOUT ALESIA AND A CERTAIN SHIELD...
ZZZZZ
ZZZZ
BE BRIEF CARPE DIEM
CALL THE GUARD!
I'VE PICKED UP THE MESSAGE, ASTERIX!
WELL DONE! NOW GO OUTSIDE THE DOOR AND STOP ANYONE COMING IN.
LUCIUS CIRCUMBENDIBUS! WHAT'S HAPPENING?
?
YOU CAN'T COME IN...
CIRCUMBENDIBUS IS IN A MEETING.
CHTONK!

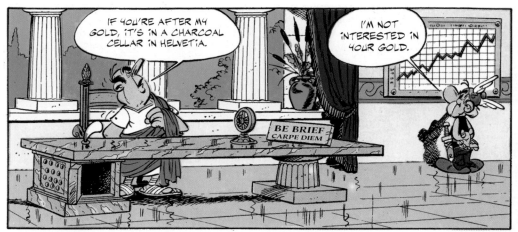

IF YOU'RE AFTER MY GOLD, IT'S IN A CHARCOAL CELLAR IN HELVETIA.

I'M NOT INTERESTED IN YOUR GOLD.

BE BRIEF
CARPE DIEM

I'VE TOLD YOU WHAT I WANT, BY TOUTATIS! THE CHIEFTAIN'S SHIELD YOU GOT AT ALESIA!

I'M A BIG WHEEL, YOU KNOW; IN MY LINE TIME IS SESTERTII, SO LET'S COME TO THE HUB OF THE MATTER. ARE YOU THREATENING ME?

YES.

I THOUGHT SO. I'LL TELL YOU EVERYTHING. I HAVEN'T GOT THE SHIELD ANY MORE...

YOU'RE RIGHT, I DID GET HOLD OF IT AFTER THE DEFEAT OF VERCINGETORIX...

...BUT IN MY YOUTH I WAS CONSUMED BY THE URGE TO GAMBLE (I JOINED THE LEGION AS THE RESULT OF A SILLY BET)...

HEY, HOW ABOUT A GAME OF RUBER ET NIGER?

!

...I LOST THE SHIELD TO A LEGIONARY CALLED MARCUS CARNIVERUS IN A GAME OF CHANCE.

DIEM PERDIDI!

YOU CAN QUOTE ME ON THAT TOO!

WHEN I WAS DEMOBBED I STAYED IN THESE PARTS AND MADE MY PILE. THE WHEEL OF FORTUNE TURNED MY WAY...

WHERE'S THIS CARNIVERUS NOW?

I THINK HE'S A BATH ATTENDANT AT THE HYDRO IN BORVO.*

BE BRIEF
CARPE DIEM

* LA BOURBOULE

?

SHE CALLED THESE PEOPLE, AND THEY WOULDN'T BELIEVE CIRCUMBENDIBUS WAS IN A MEETING, SO I HAD TO DEAL WITH THEM. LOOK, NO HANDS!

31

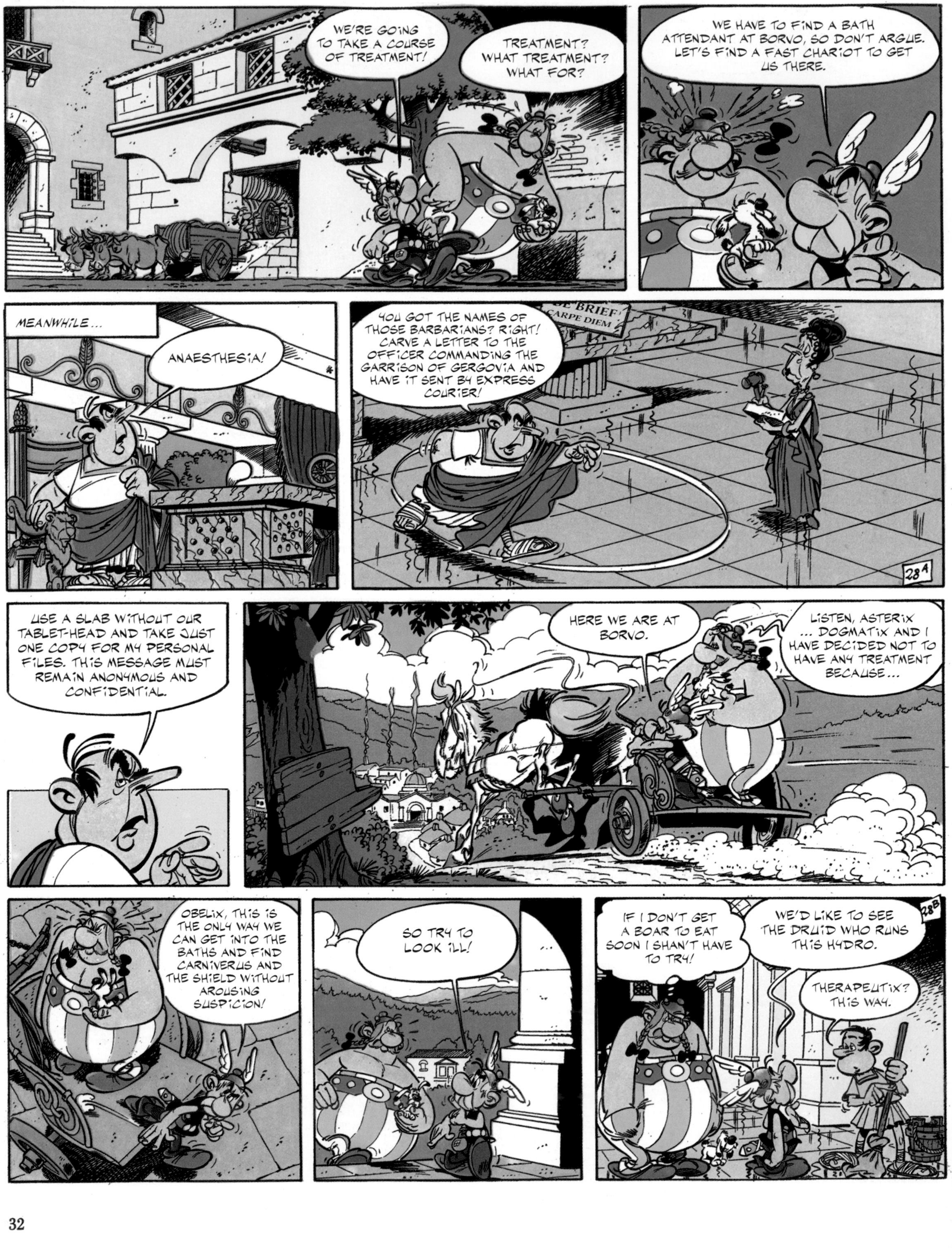
WE'RE GOING TO TAKE A COURSE OF TREATMENT!
TREATMENT? WHAT TREATMENT? WHAT FOR?
WE HAVE TO FIND A BATH ATTENDANT AT BORVO, SO DON'T ARGUE. LET'S FIND A FAST CHARIOT TO GET US THERE.
MEANWHILE...
ANAESTHESIA!
CARPE DIEM
YOU GOT THE NAMES OF THOSE BARBARIANS? RIGHT! CARVE A LETTER TO THE OFFICER COMMANDING THE GARRISON OF GERGOVIA AND HAVE IT SENT BY EXPRESS COURIER!
28A
USE A SLAB WITHOUT OUR TABLET-HEAD AND TAKE JUST ONE COPY FOR MY PERSONAL FILES. THIS MESSAGE MUST REMAIN ANONYMOUS AND CONFIDENTIAL.
HERE WE ARE AT BORVO.
LISTEN, ASTERIX ... DOGMATIX AND I HAVE DECIDED NOT TO HAVE ANY TREATMENT BECAUSE...
OBELIX, THIS IS THE ONLY WAY WE CAN GET INTO THE BATHS AND FIND CARNIVERUS AND THE SHIELD WITHOUT AROUSING SUSPICION!
SO TRY TO LOOK ILL!
IF I DON'T GET A BOAR TO EAT SOON I SHAN'T HAVE TO TRY!
28B
WE'D LIKE TO SEE THE DRUID WHO RUNS THIS HYDRO.
THERAPEUTIX? THIS WAY.

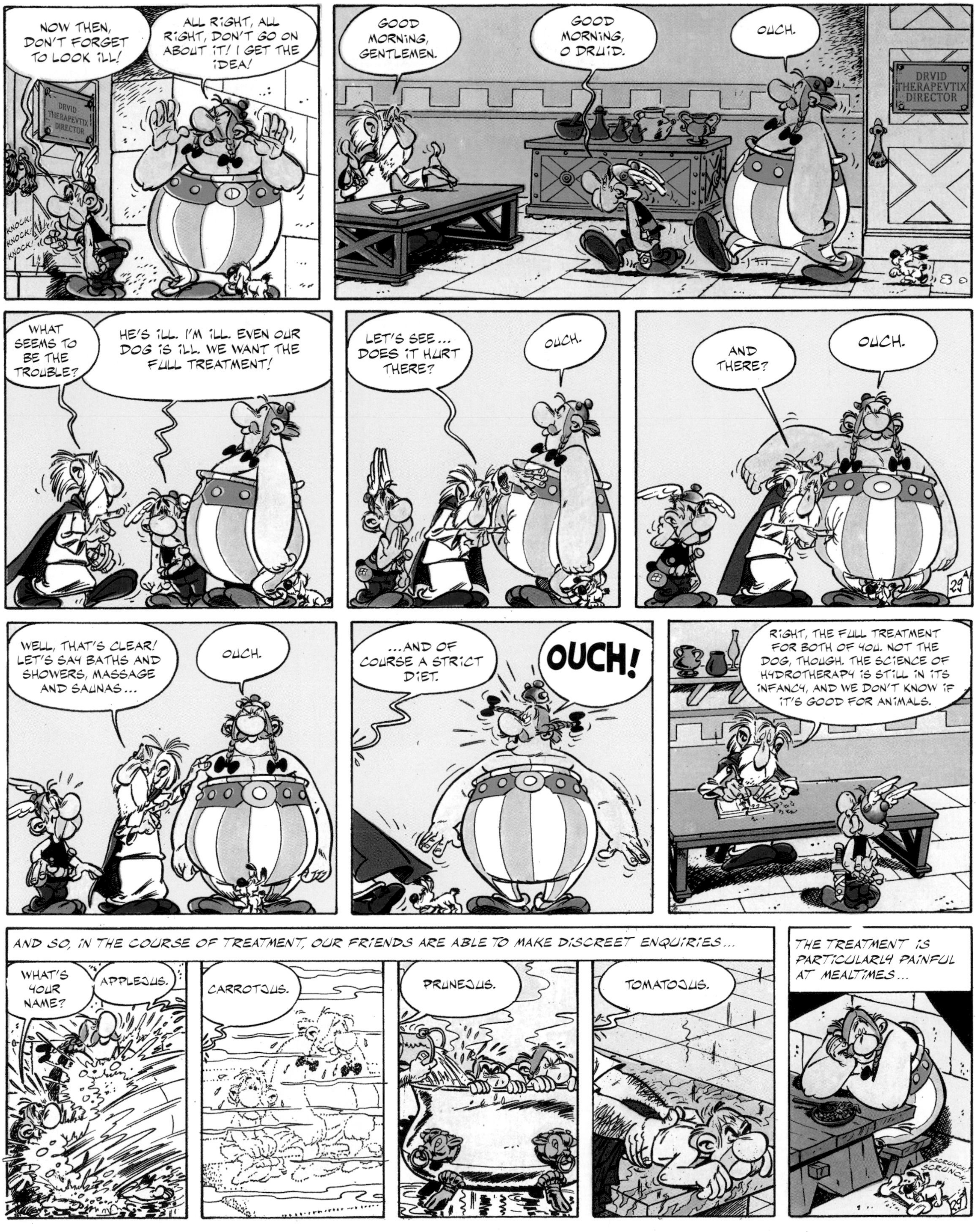
NOW THEN, DON'T FORGET TO LOOK ILL!
ALL RIGHT, ALL RIGHT, DON'T GO ON ABOUT IT! I GET THE IDEA!
DRVID THERAPEVTIX DIRECTOR
KNOCK! KNOCK! KNOCK!
GOOD MORNING, GENTLEMEN.
GOOD MORNING, O DRUID.
OUCH.
DRVID THERAPEVTIX DIRECTOR
WHAT SEEMS TO BE THE TROUBLE?
HE'S ILL. I'M ILL. EVEN OUR DOG IS ILL. WE WANT THE FULL TREATMENT!
LET'S SEE... DOES IT HURT THERE?
OUCH.
AND THERE?
OUCH.
WELL, THAT'S CLEAR! LET'S SAY BATHS AND SHOWERS, MASSAGE AND SAUNAS...
OUCH.
...AND OF COURSE A STRICT DIET.
OUCH!
RIGHT, THE FULL TREATMENT FOR BOTH OF YOU. NOT THE DOG, THOUGH. THE SCIENCE OF HYDROTHERAPY IS STILL IN ITS INFANCY, AND WE DON'T KNOW IF IT'S GOOD FOR ANIMALS.
AND SO, IN THE COURSE OF TREATMENT, OUR FRIENDS ARE ABLE TO MAKE DISCREET ENQUIRIES...
WHAT'S YOUR NAME?
APPLEJUS.
CARROTJUS.
PRUNEJUS.
TOMATOJUS.
THE TREATMENT IS PARTICULARLY PAINFUL AT MEALTIMES...
SCRUNCH! SCRUNCH!

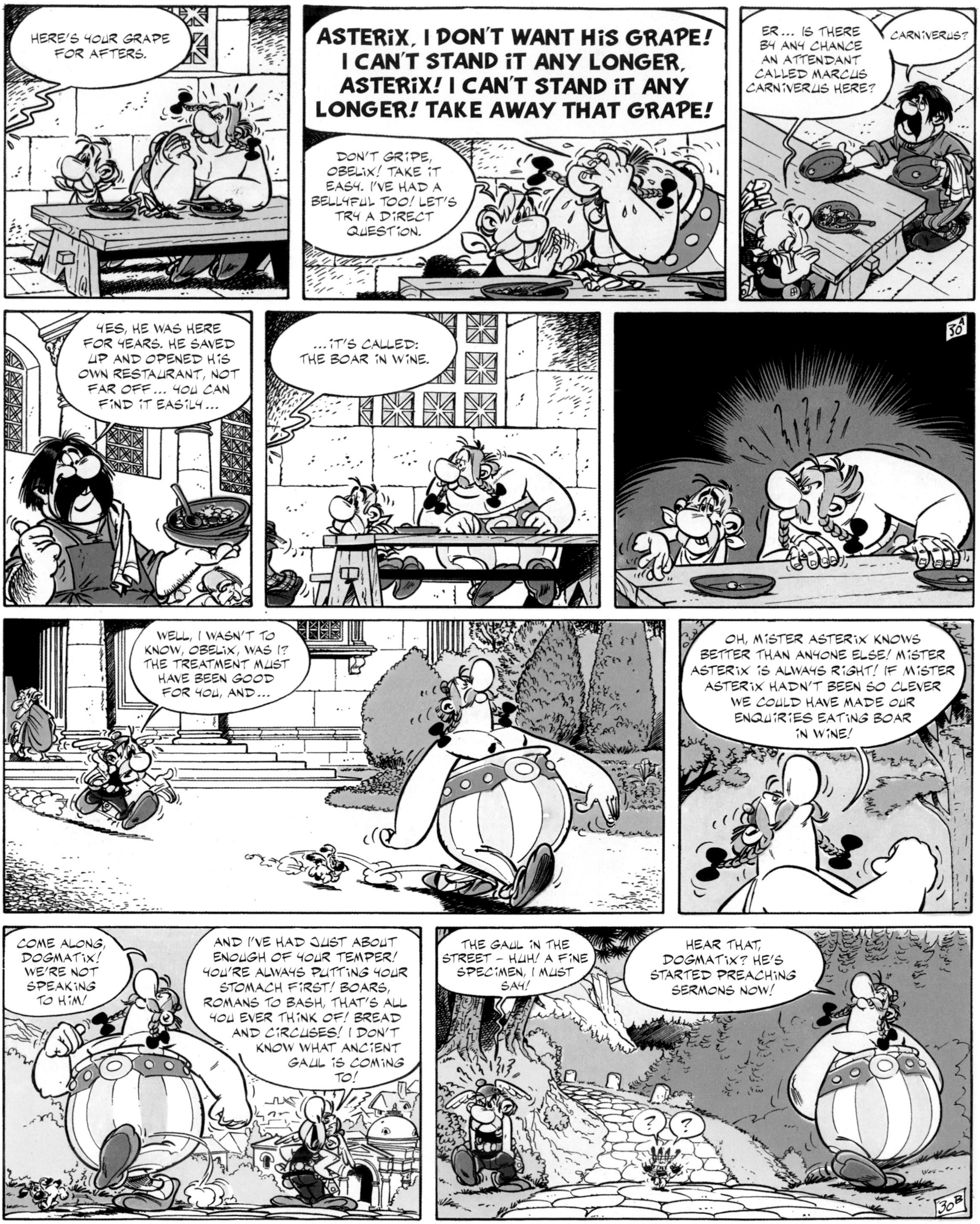
HERE'S YOUR GRAPE FOR AFTERS.
ASTERIX, I DON'T WANT HIS GRAPE! I CAN'T STAND IT ANY LONGER, ASTERIX! I CAN'T STAND IT ANY LONGER! TAKE AWAY THAT GRAPE!
DON'T GRIPE, OBELIX! TAKE IT EASY. I'VE HAD A BELLYFUL TOO! LET'S TRY A DIRECT QUESTION.
ER... IS THERE BY ANY CHANCE AN ATTENDANT CALLED MARCUS CARNIVERUS HERE?
CARNIVERUS?
YES, HE WAS HERE FOR YEARS. HE SAVED UP AND OPENED HIS OWN RESTAURANT, NOT FAR OFF... YOU CAN FIND IT EASILY...
...IT'S CALLED: THE BOAR IN WINE.
30A
WELL, I WASN'T TO KNOW, OBELIX, WAS I? THE TREATMENT MUST HAVE BEEN GOOD FOR YOU, AND...
OH, MISTER ASTERIX KNOWS BETTER THAN ANYONE ELSE! MISTER ASTERIX IS ALWAYS RIGHT! IF MISTER ASTERIX HADN'T BEEN SO CLEVER WE COULD HAVE MADE OUR ENQUIRIES EATING BOAR IN WINE!
COME ALONG, DOGMATIX! WE'RE NOT SPEAKING TO HIM!
AND I'VE HAD JUST ABOUT ENOUGH OF YOUR TEMPER! YOU'RE ALWAYS PUTTING YOUR STOMACH FIRST! BOARS, ROMANS TO BASH, THAT'S ALL YOU EVER THINK OF! BREAD AND CIRCUSES! I DON'T KNOW WHAT ANCIENT GAUL IS COMING TO!
THE GAUL IN THE STREET – HUH! A FINE SPECIMEN, I MUST SAY!
HEAR THAT, DOGMATIX? HE'S STARTED PREACHING SERMONS NOW!
? ?
30B

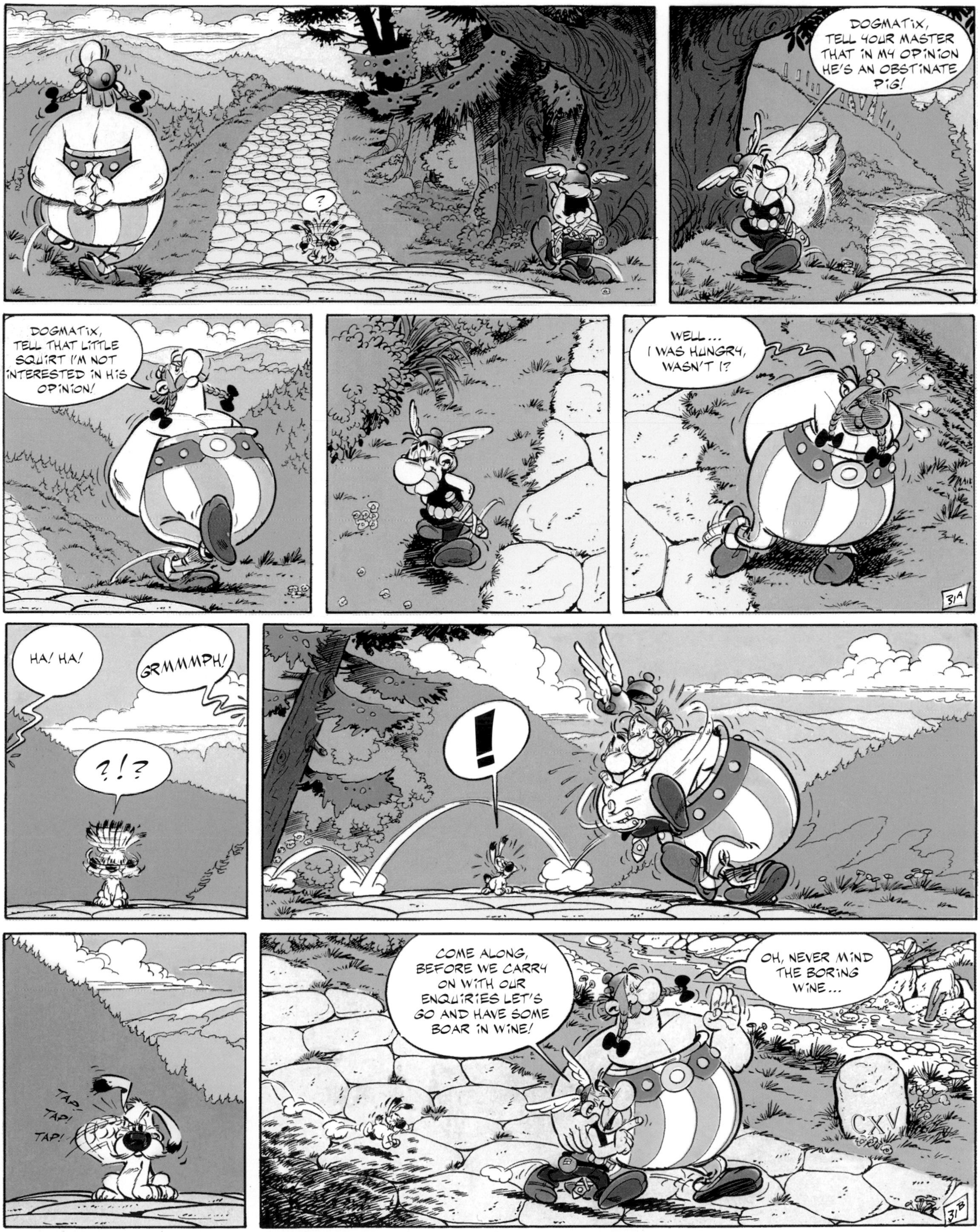
?
DOGMATIX, TELL YOUR MASTER THAT IN MY OPINION HE'S AN OBSTINATE PIG!
DOGMATIX, TELL THAT LITTLE SQUIRT I'M NOT INTERESTED IN HIS OPINION!
WELL... I WAS HUNGRY, WASN'T I?
31A
HA! HA!
GRMMMPH!
?!?
!
TAP!
TAP!
TAP!
COME ALONG, BEFORE WE CARRY ON WITH OUR ENQUIRIES LET'S GO AND HAVE SOME BOAR IN WINE!
OH, NEVER MIND THE BORING WINE...
CXV
31B

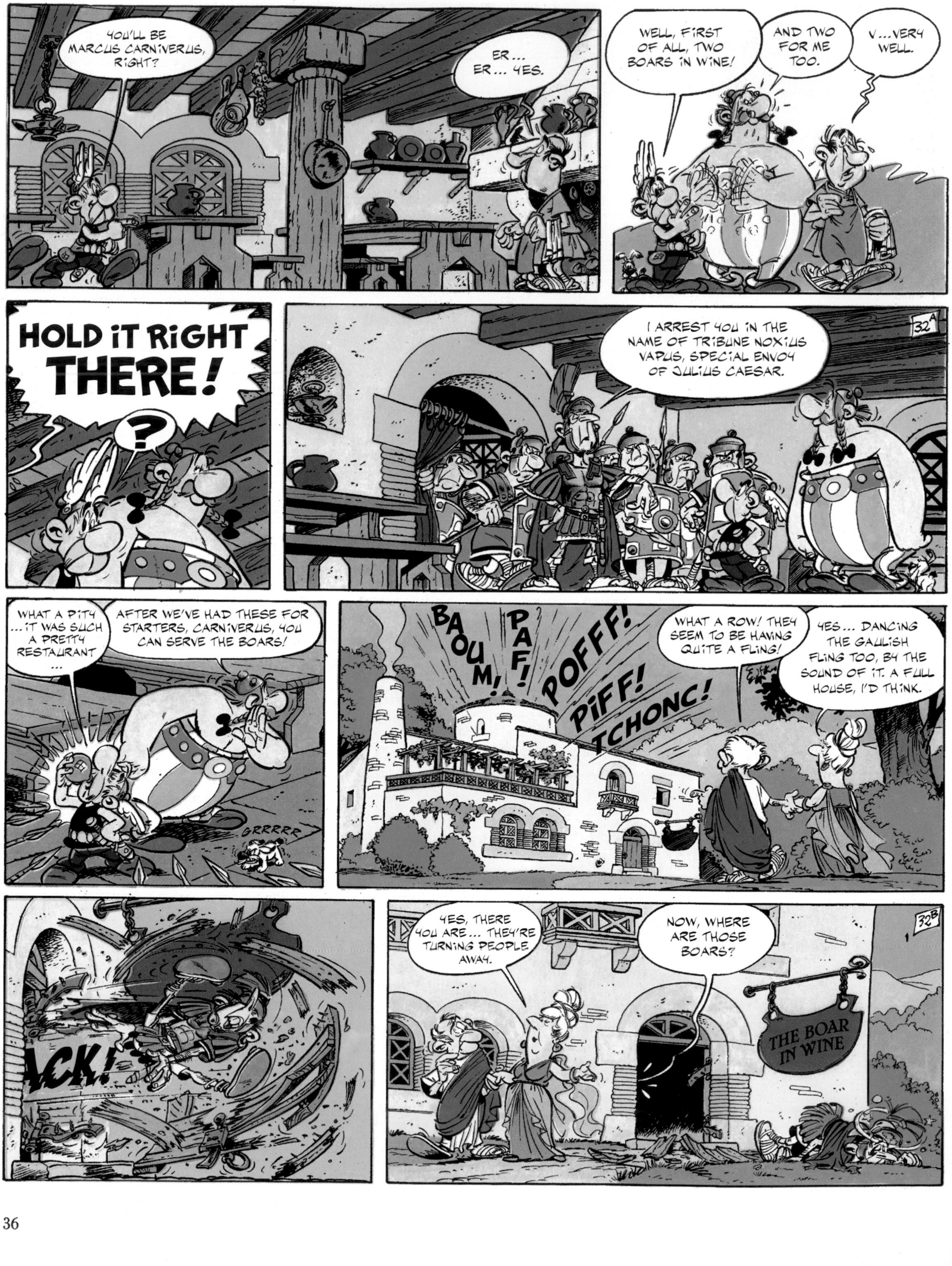

YOU'LL BE MARCUS CARNIVERUS, RIGHT?
ER... ER... YES.
WELL, FIRST OF ALL, TWO BOARS IN WINE!
AND TWO FOR ME TOO.
V...VERY WELL.
HOLD IT RIGHT THERE!
?
I ARREST YOU IN THE NAME OF TRIBUNE NOXIUS VAPUS, SPECIAL ENVOY OF JULIUS CAESAR.
32A
WHAT A PITY ...IT WAS SUCH A PRETTY RESTAURANT ...
AFTER WE'VE HAD THESE FOR STARTERS, CARNIVERUS, YOU CAN SERVE THE BOARS!
GRRRRR
BAOUM!
PAF!
POFFF!
PIFF!
TCHONC!
WHAT A ROW! THEY SEEM TO BE HAVING QUITE A FLING!
YES... DANCING THE GAULISH FLING TOO, BY THE SOUND OF IT. A FULL HOUSE, I'D THINK.
ACK!
YES, THERE YOU ARE... THEY'RE TURNING PEOPLE AWAY.
NOW, WHERE ARE THOSE BOARS?
THE BOAR IN WINE
32B

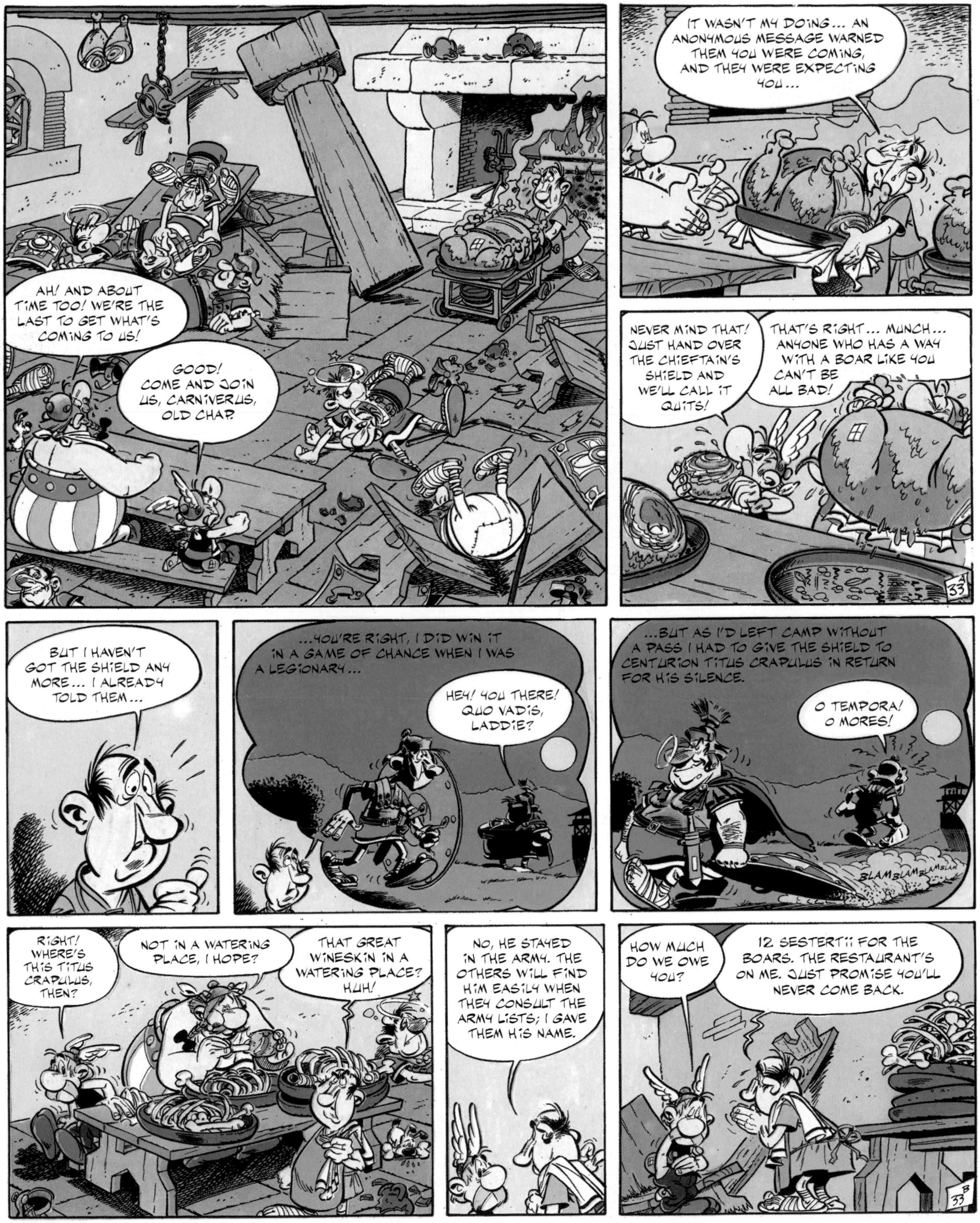
AH! AND ABOUT TIME TOO! WE'RE THE LAST TO GET WHAT'S COMING TO US!
GOOD! COME AND JOIN US, CARNIVERUS, OLD CHAP.
IT WASN'T MY DOING... AN ANONYMOUS MESSAGE WARNED THEM YOU WERE COMING, AND THEY WERE EXPECTING YOU...
NEVER MIND THAT! JUST HAND OVER THE CHIEFTAIN'S SHIELD AND WE'LL CALL IT QUITS!
THAT'S RIGHT... MUNCH... ANYONE WHO HAS A WAY WITH A BOAR LIKE YOU CAN'T BE ALL BAD!
33A
BUT I HAVEN'T GOT THE SHIELD ANY MORE... I ALREADY TOLD THEM...
...YOU'RE RIGHT, I DID WIN IT IN A GAME OF CHANCE WHEN I WAS A LEGIONARY...
HEY! YOU THERE! QUO VADIS, LADDIE?
...BUT AS I'D LEFT CAMP WITHOUT A PASS I HAD TO GIVE THE SHIELD TO CENTURION TITUS CRAPULUS IN RETURN FOR HIS SILENCE.
O TEMPORA! O MORES!
BLAM BLAM BLAM BLAM
RIGHT! WHERE'S THIS TITUS CRAPULUS, THEN?
NOT IN A WATERING PLACE, I HOPE?
THAT GREAT WINESKIN IN A WATERING PLACE? HUH!
NO, HE STAYED IN THE ARMY. THE OTHERS WILL FIND HIM EASILY WHEN THEY CONSULT THE ARMY LISTS; I GAVE THEM HIS NAME.
HOW MUCH DO WE OWE YOU?
12 SESTERTII FOR THE BOARS. THE RESTAURANT'S ON ME. JUST PROMISE YOU'LL NEVER COME BACK.
33B

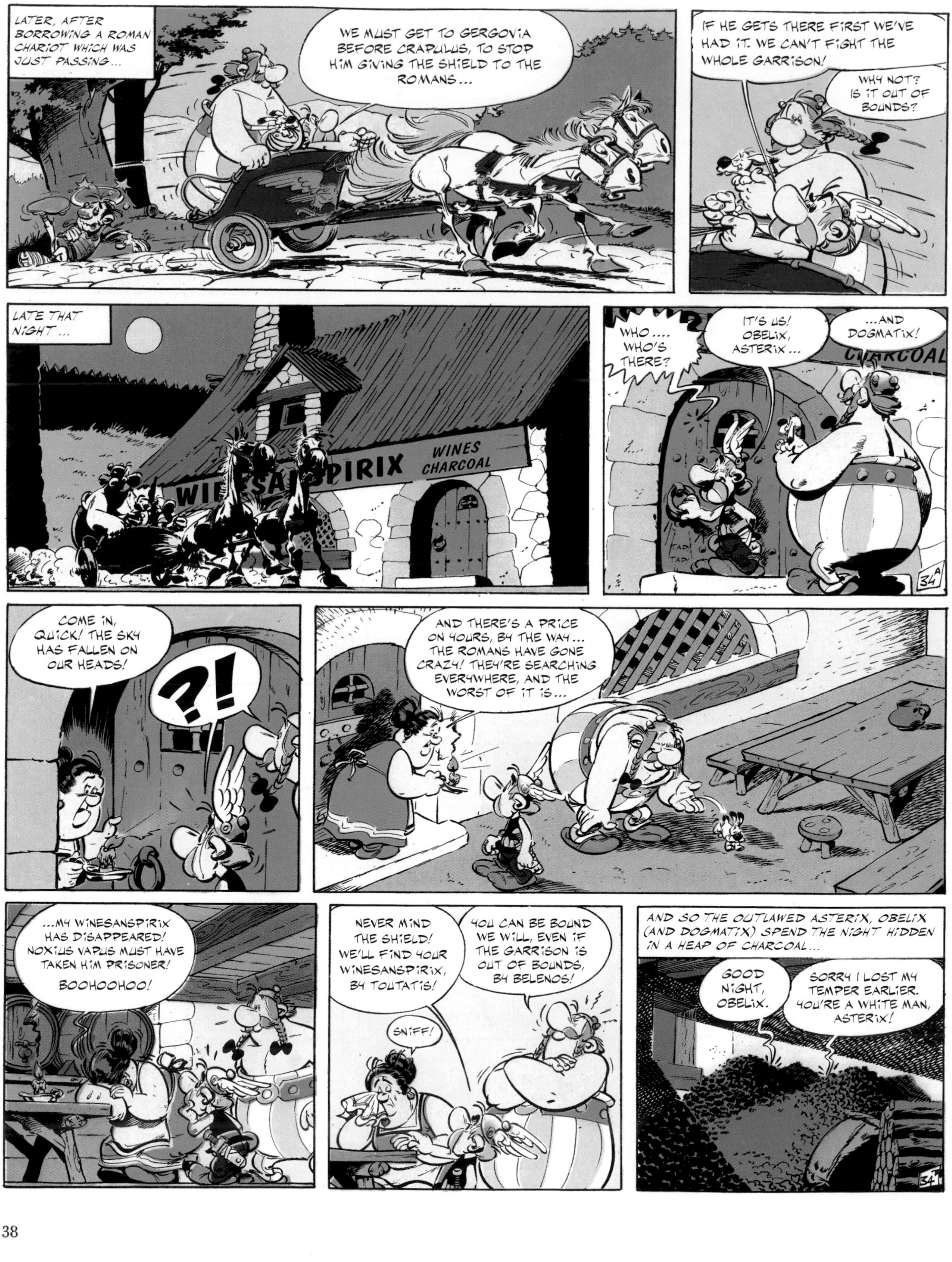

LATER, AFTER BORROWING A ROMAN CHARIOT WHICH WAS JUST PASSING...
WE MUST GET TO GERGOVIA BEFORE CRAPULUS, TO STOP HIM GIVING THE SHIELD TO THE ROMANS...
IF HE GETS THERE FIRST WE'VE HAD IT. WE CAN'T FIGHT THE WHOLE GARRISON!
WHY NOT? IS IT OUT OF BOUNDS?
LATE THAT NIGHT...
WINESANSPIRIX
WINES CHARCOAL
WHO.... WHO'S THERE?
IT'S US! OBELIX, ASTERIX...
...AND DOGMATIX!
COME IN, QUICK! THE SKY HAS FALLEN ON OUR HEADS!
?!
AND THERE'S A PRICE ON YOURS, BY THE WAY... THE ROMANS HAVE GONE CRAZY! THEY'RE SEARCHING EVERYWHERE, AND THE WORST OF IT IS...
...MY WINESANSPIRIX HAS DISAPPEARED! NOXIUS VAPUS MUST HAVE TAKEN HIM PRISONER!
BOOHOOHOO!
NEVER MIND THE SHIELD! WE'LL FIND YOUR WINESANSPIRIX, BY TOUTATIS!
YOU CAN BE BOUND WE WILL, EVEN IF THE GARRISON IS OUT OF BOUNDS, BY BELENOS!
SNIFF!
AND SO THE OUTLAWED ASTERIX, OBELIX (AND DOGMATIX) SPEND THE NIGHT HIDDEN IN A HEAP OF CHARCOAL...
GOOD NIGHT, OBELIX.
SORRY I LOST MY TEMPER EARLIER. YOU'RE A WHITE MAN, ASTERIX!

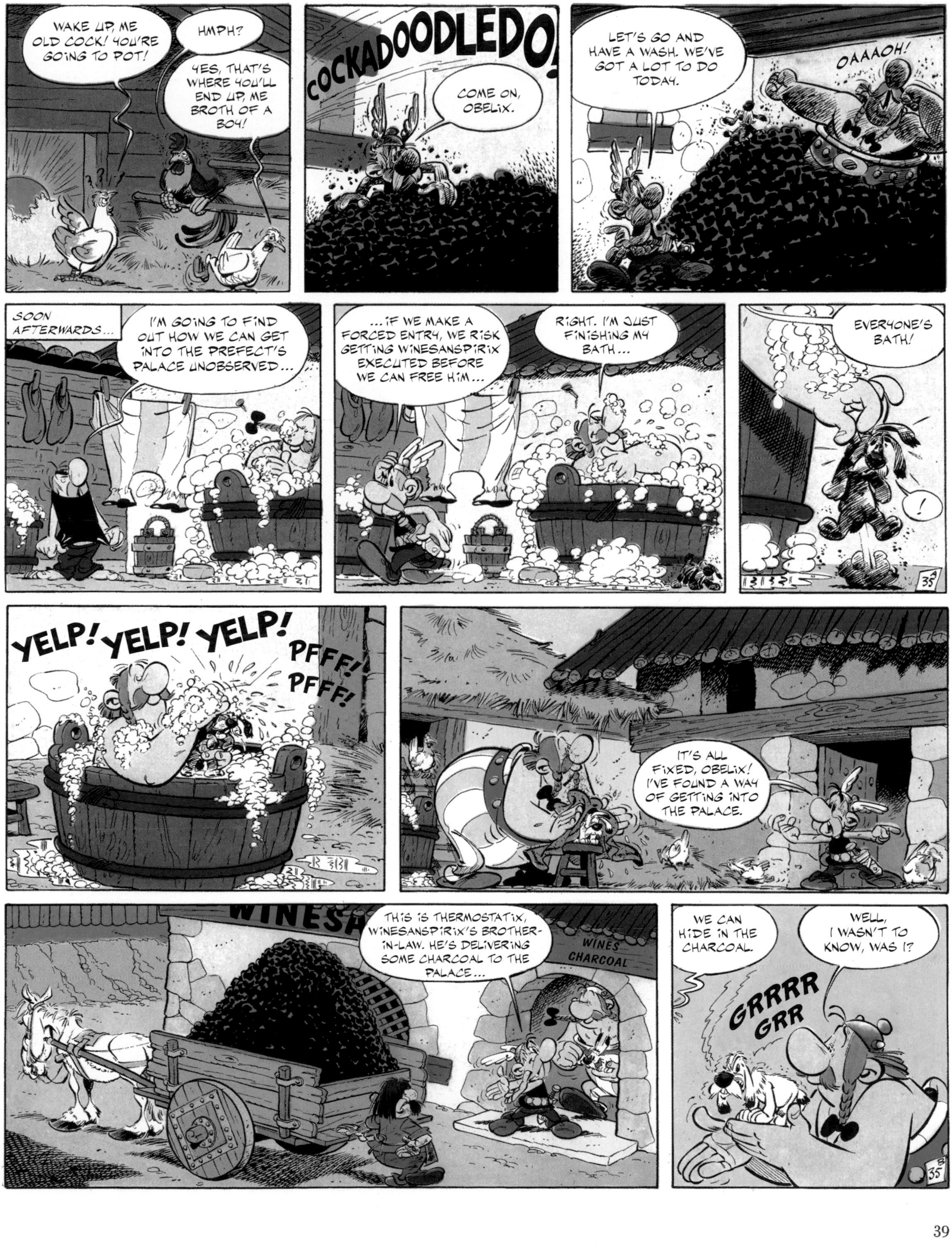
WAKE UP, ME OLD COCK! YOU'RE GOING TO POT!
HMPH?
YES, THAT'S WHERE YOU'LL END UP, ME BROTH OF A BOY!
COCKADOODLEDO!
COME ON, OBELIX.
LET'S GO AND HAVE A WASH. WE'VE GOT A LOT TO DO TODAY.
OAAAOH!
SOON AFTERWARDS...
I'M GOING TO FIND OUT HOW WE CAN GET INTO THE PREFECT'S PALACE UNOBSERVED...
...IF WE MAKE A FORCED ENTRY, WE RISK GETTING WINESANSPIRIX EXECUTED BEFORE WE CAN FREE HIM...
RIGHT. I'M JUST FINISHING MY BATH...
EVERYONE'S BATH!
!
YELP! YELP! YELP!
PFFF! PFFF!
IT'S ALL FIXED, OBELIX! I'VE FOUND A WAY OF GETTING INTO THE PALACE.
WINESA
WINES CHARCOAL
THIS IS THERMOSTATIX, WINESANSPIRIX'S BROTHER-IN-LAW. HE'S DELIVERING SOME CHARCOAL TO THE PALACE...
WE CAN HIDE IN THE CHARCOAL.
WELL, I WASN'T TO KNOW, WAS I?
GRRRR GRR

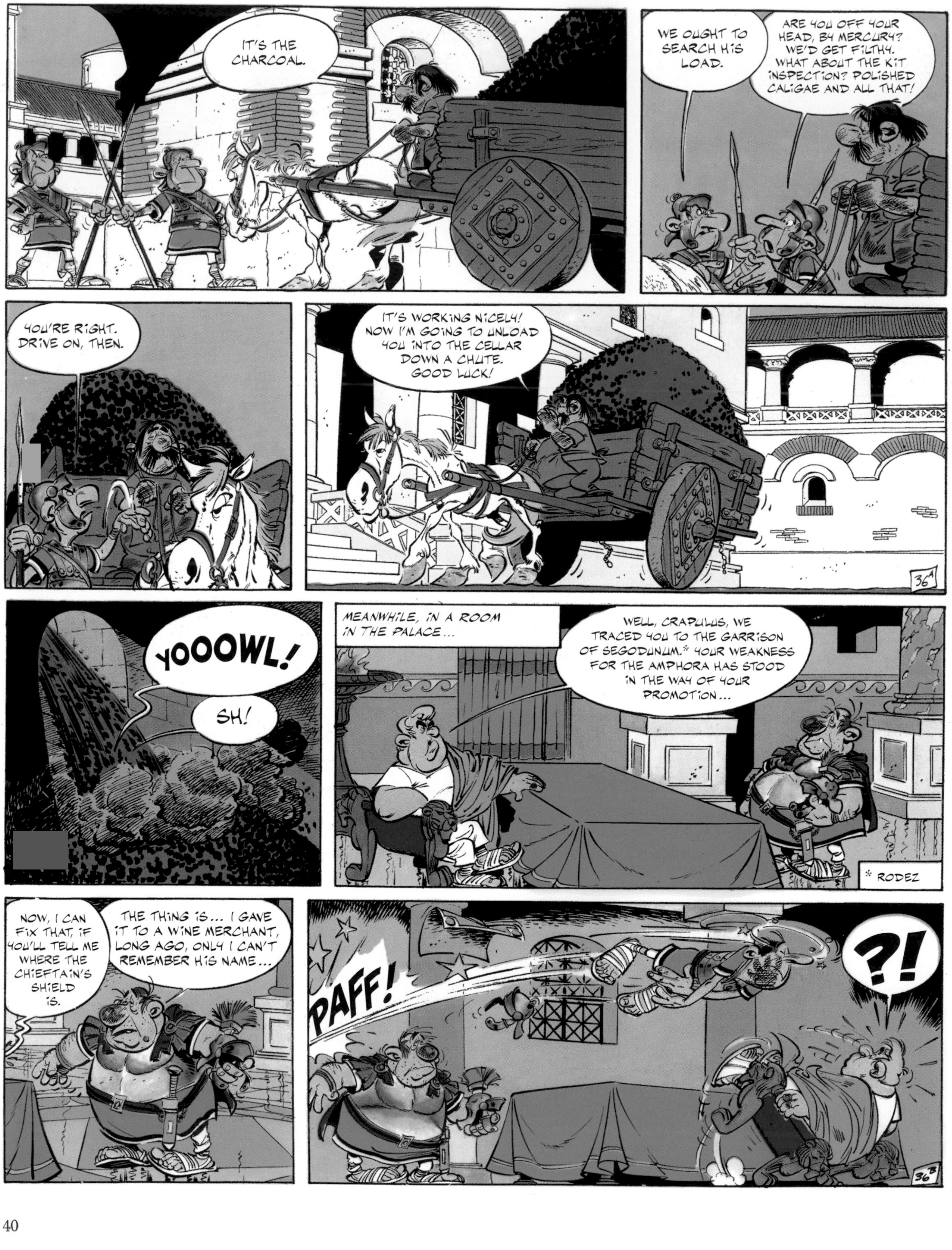
IT'S THE CHARCOAL.
WE OUGHT TO SEARCH HIS LOAD.
ARE YOU OFF YOUR HEAD, BY MERCURY? WE'D GET FILTHY. WHAT ABOUT THE KIT INSPECTION? POLISHED CALIGAE AND ALL THAT!
YOU'RE RIGHT. DRIVE ON, THEN.
IT'S WORKING NICELY! NOW I'M GOING TO UNLOAD YOU INTO THE CELLAR DOWN A CHUTE. GOOD LUCK!
36A
YOOOWL!
SH!
MEANWHILE, IN A ROOM IN THE PALACE...
WELL, CRAPULUS, WE TRACED YOU TO THE GARRISON OF SEGODUNUM.* YOUR WEAKNESS FOR THE AMPHORA HAS STOOD IN THE WAY OF YOUR PROMOTION...
* RODEZ
NOW, I CAN FIX THAT, IF YOU'LL TELL ME WHERE THE CHIEFTAIN'S SHIELD IS.
THE THING IS... I GAVE IT TO A WINE MERCHANT, LONG AGO, ONLY I CAN'T REMEMBER HIS NAME...
PAFF!
?!
36B

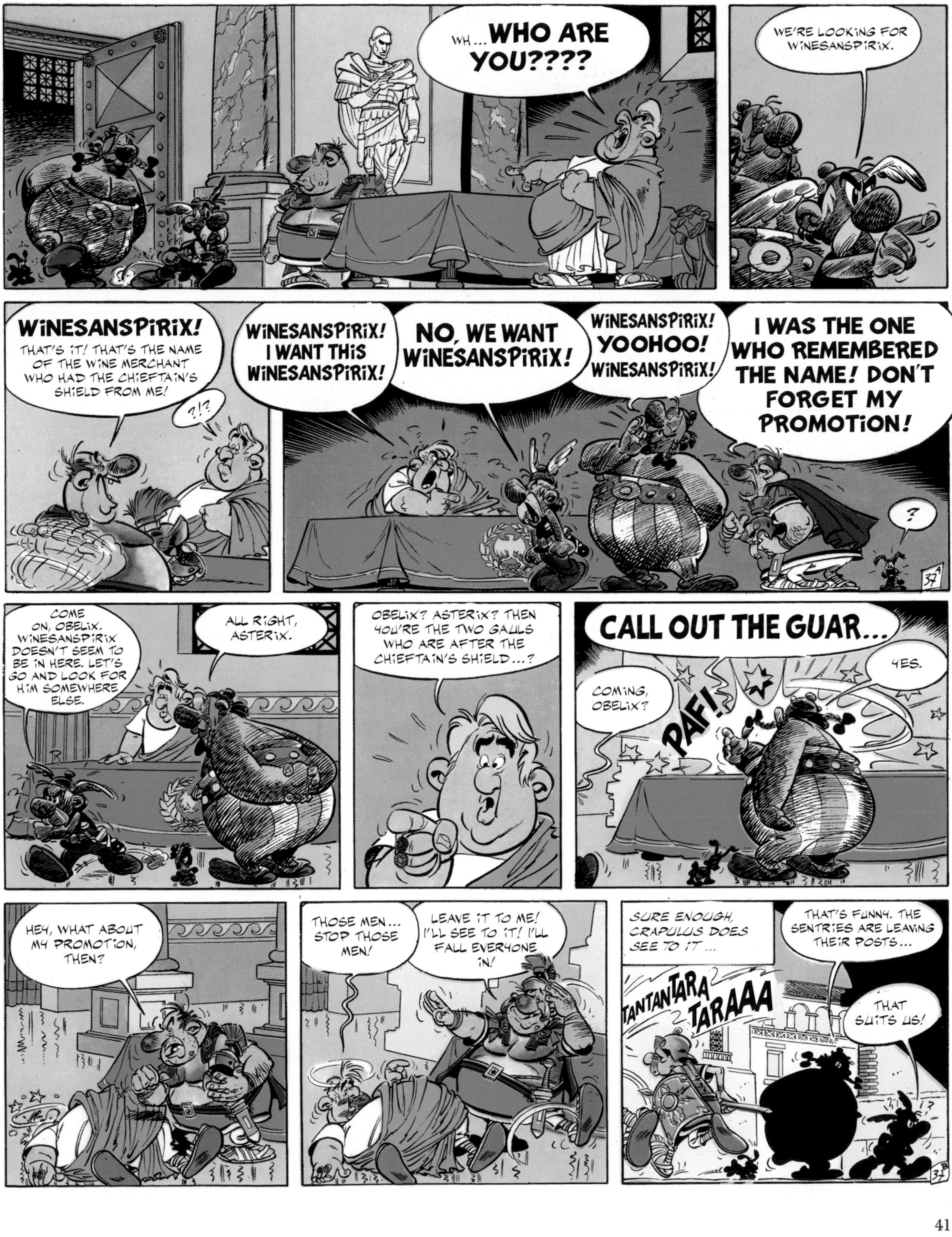
WH... WHO ARE YOU????
WE'RE LOOKING FOR WINESANSPIRIX.
WINESANSPIRIX! THAT'S IT! THAT'S THE NAME OF THE WINE MERCHANT WHO HAD THE CHIEFTAIN'S SHIELD FROM ME!
?!?
WINESANSPIRIX! I WANT THIS WINESANSPIRIX!
NO, WE WANT WINESANSPIRIX!
WINESANSPIRIX! YOOHOO! WINESANSPIRIX!
I WAS THE ONE WHO REMEMBERED THE NAME! DON'T FORGET MY PROMOTION!
?
COME ON, OBELIX. WINESANSPIRIX DOESN'T SEEM TO BE IN HERE. LET'S GO AND LOOK FOR HIM SOMEWHERE ELSE.
ALL RIGHT, ASTERIX.
OBELIX? ASTERIX? THEN YOU'RE THE TWO GAULS WHO ARE AFTER THE CHIEFTAIN'S SHIELD...?
CALL OUT THE GUAR...
COMING, OBELIX?
YES.
PAF!
HEY, WHAT ABOUT MY PROMOTION, THEN?
THOSE MEN... STOP THOSE MEN!
LEAVE IT TO ME! I'LL SEE TO IT! I'LL FALL EVERYONE IN!
SURE ENOUGH, CRAPULUS DOES SEE TO IT...
TANTANTARA TARAAA
THAT'S FUNNY. THE SENTRIES ARE LEAVING THEIR POSTS...
THAT SUITS US!
!?

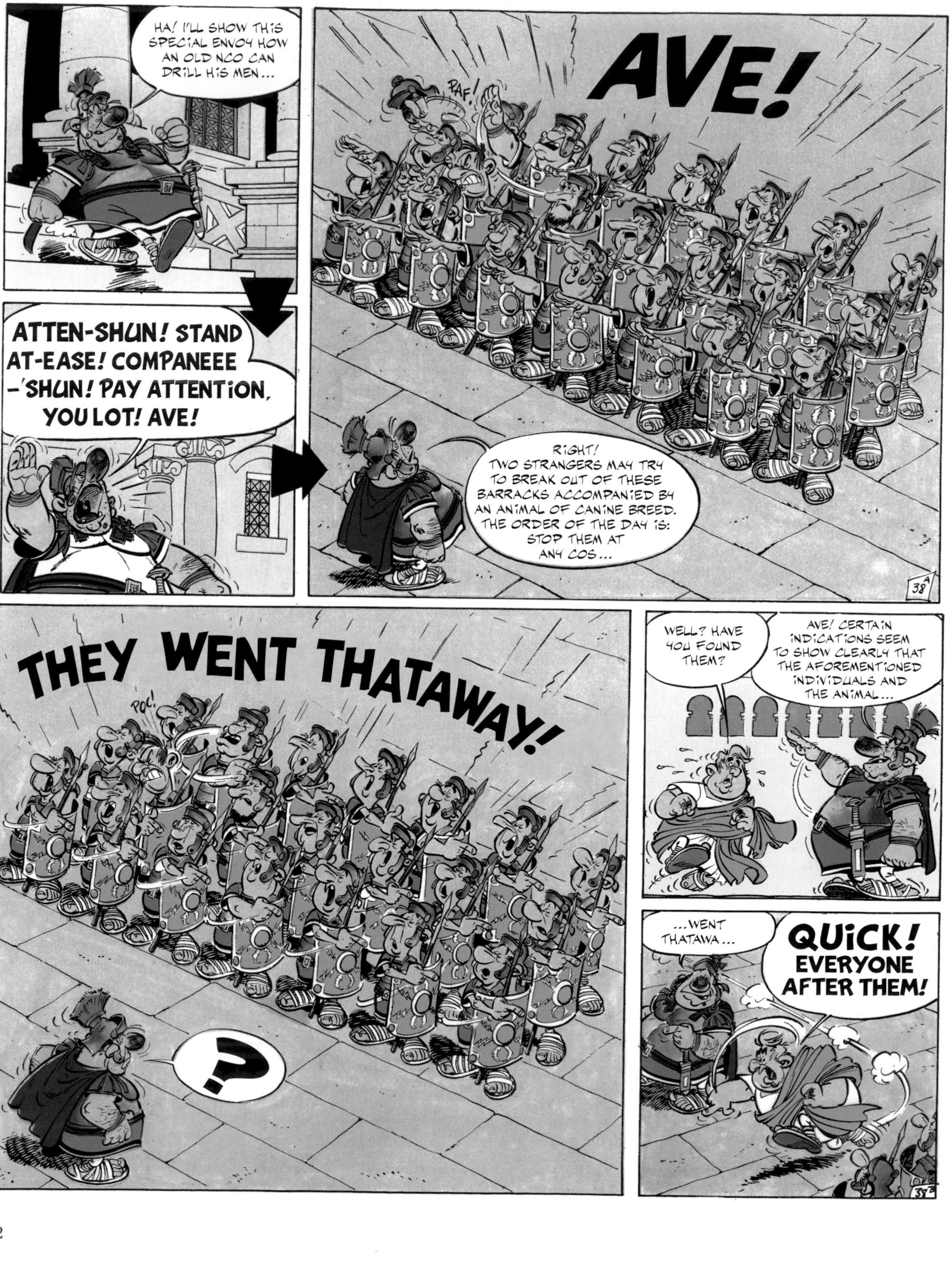
HA! I'LL SHOW THIS SPECIAL ENVOY HOW AN OLD NCO CAN DRILL HIS MEN...
ATTEN-SHUN! STAND AT-EASE! COMPANEEE -'SHUN! PAY ATTENTION, YOU LOT! AVE!
PAF!
AVE!
RIGHT! TWO STRANGERS MAY TRY TO BREAK OUT OF THESE BARRACKS ACCOMPANIED BY AN ANIMAL OF CANINE BREED. THE ORDER OF THE DAY IS: STOP THEM AT ANY COS...
POC!
THEY WENT THATAWAY!
?
WELL? HAVE YOU FOUND THEM?
AVE! CERTAIN INDICATIONS SEEM TO SHOW CLEARLY THAT THE AFOREMENTIONED INDIVIDUALS AND THE ANIMAL...
...WENT THATAWA...
QUICK! EVERYONE AFTER THEM!

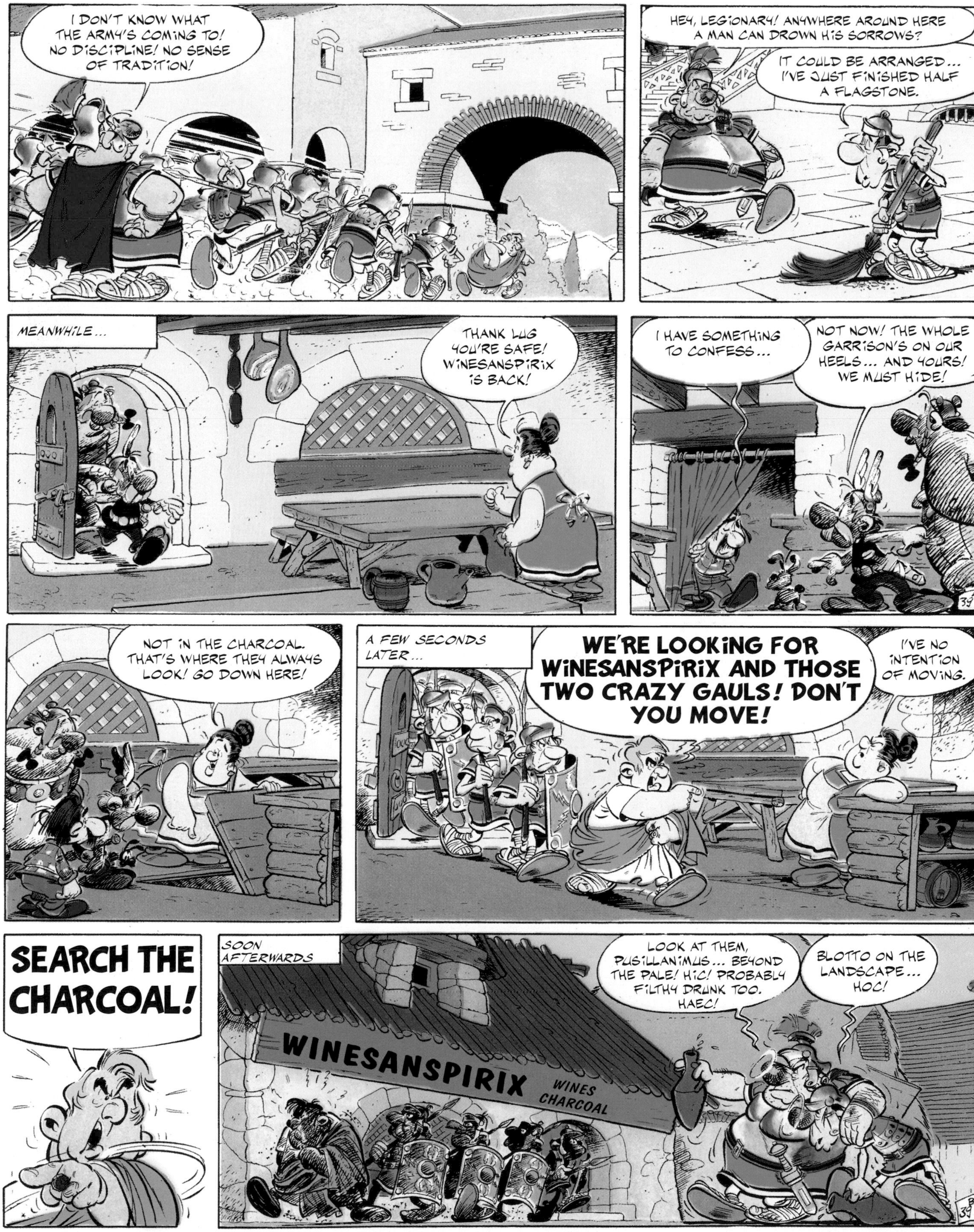
I DON'T KNOW WHAT THE ARMY'S COMING TO! NO DISCIPLINE! NO SENSE OF TRADITION!
HEY, LEGIONARY! ANYWHERE AROUND HERE A MAN CAN DROWN HIS SORROWS?
IT COULD BE ARRANGED... I'VE JUST FINISHED HALF A FLAGSTONE.
MEANWHILE...
THANK LUG YOU'RE SAFE! WINESANSPIRIX IS BACK!
I HAVE SOMETHING TO CONFESS...
NOT NOW! THE WHOLE GARRISON'S ON OUR HEELS... AND YOURS! WE MUST HIDE!
NOT IN THE CHARCOAL. THAT'S WHERE THEY ALWAYS LOOK! GO DOWN HERE!
A FEW SECONDS LATER...
WE'RE LOOKING FOR WINESANSPIRIX AND THOSE TWO CRAZY GAULS! DON'T YOU MOVE!
I'VE NO INTENTION OF MOVING.
SEARCH THE CHARCOAL!
SOON AFTERWARDS
WINESANSPIRIX WINES CHARCOAL
LOOK AT THEM, PUSILLANIMUS... BEYOND THE PALE! HIC! PROBABLY FILTHY DRUNK TOO. HAEC!
BLOTTO ON THE LANDSCAPE... HOC!

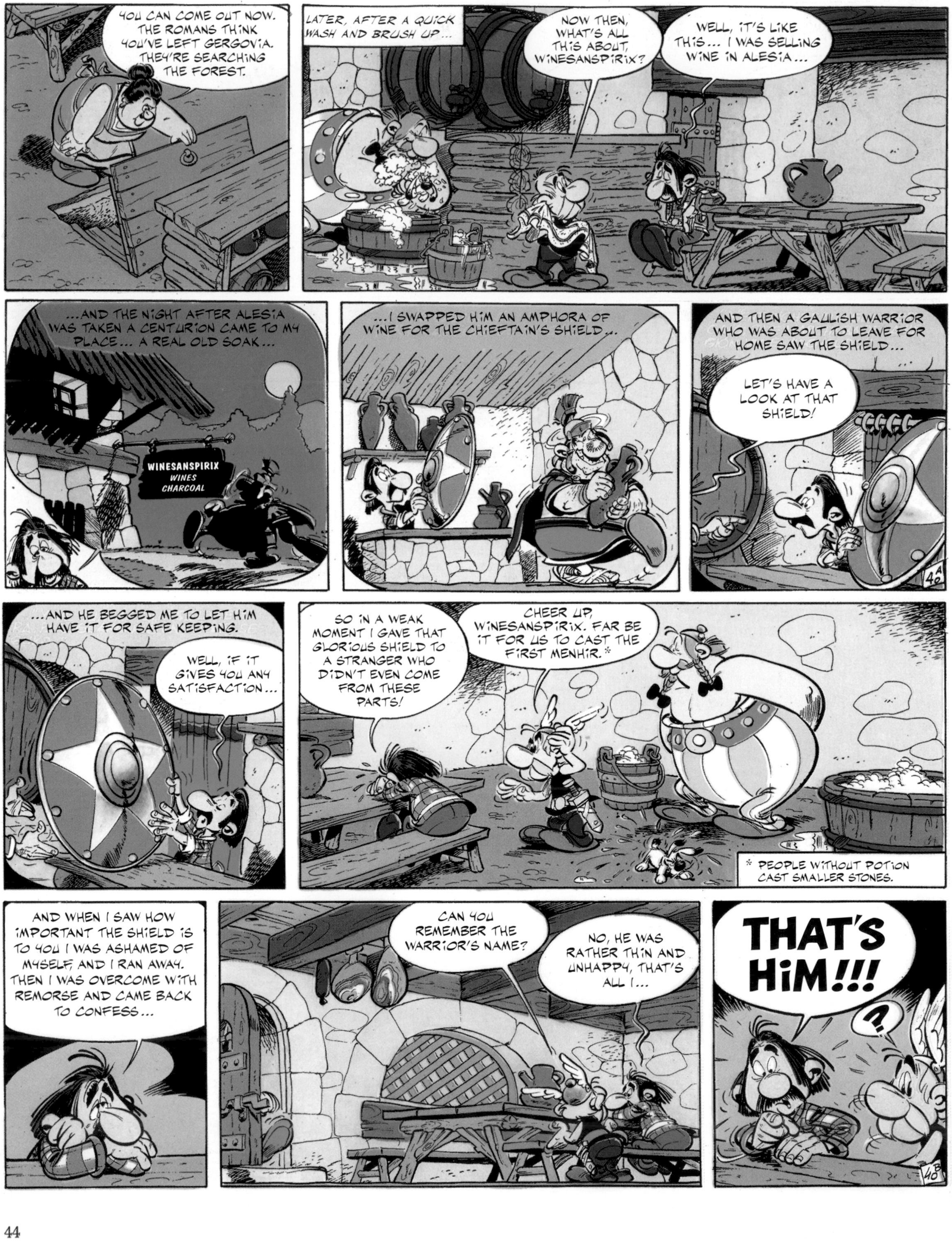
YOU CAN COME OUT NOW. THE ROMANS THINK YOU'VE LEFT GERGOVIA. THEY'RE SEARCHING THE FOREST.
LATER, AFTER A QUICK WASH AND BRUSH UP...
NOW THEN, WHAT'S ALL THIS ABOUT, WINESANSPIRIX?
WELL, IT'S LIKE THIS... I WAS SELLING WINE IN ALESIA...
...AND THE NIGHT AFTER ALESIA WAS TAKEN A CENTURION CAME TO MY PLACE... A REAL OLD SOAK...
WINESANSPIRIX
WINES
CHARCOAL
...I SWAPPED HIM AN AMPHORA OF WINE FOR THE CHIEFTAIN'S SHIELD...
AND THEN A GAULISH WARRIOR WHO WAS ABOUT TO LEAVE FOR HOME SAW THE SHIELD...
LET'S HAVE A LOOK AT THAT SHIELD!
...AND HE BEGGED ME TO LET HIM HAVE IT FOR SAFE KEEPING.
WELL, IF IT GIVES YOU ANY SATISFACTION...
SO IN A WEAK MOMENT I GAVE THAT GLORIOUS SHIELD TO A STRANGER WHO DIDN'T EVEN COME FROM THESE PARTS!
CHEER UP, WINESANSPIRIX. FAR BE IT FOR US TO CAST THE FIRST MENHIR.*
* PEOPLE WITHOUT POTION CAST SMALLER STONES.
AND WHEN I SAW HOW IMPORTANT THE SHIELD IS TO YOU I WAS ASHAMED OF MYSELF, AND I RAN AWAY. THEN I WAS OVERCOME WITH REMORSE AND CAME BACK TO CONFESS...
CAN YOU REMEMBER THE WARRIOR'S NAME?
NO, HE WAS RATHER THIN AND UNHAPPY, THAT'S ALL I...
THAT'S HIM!!!
?

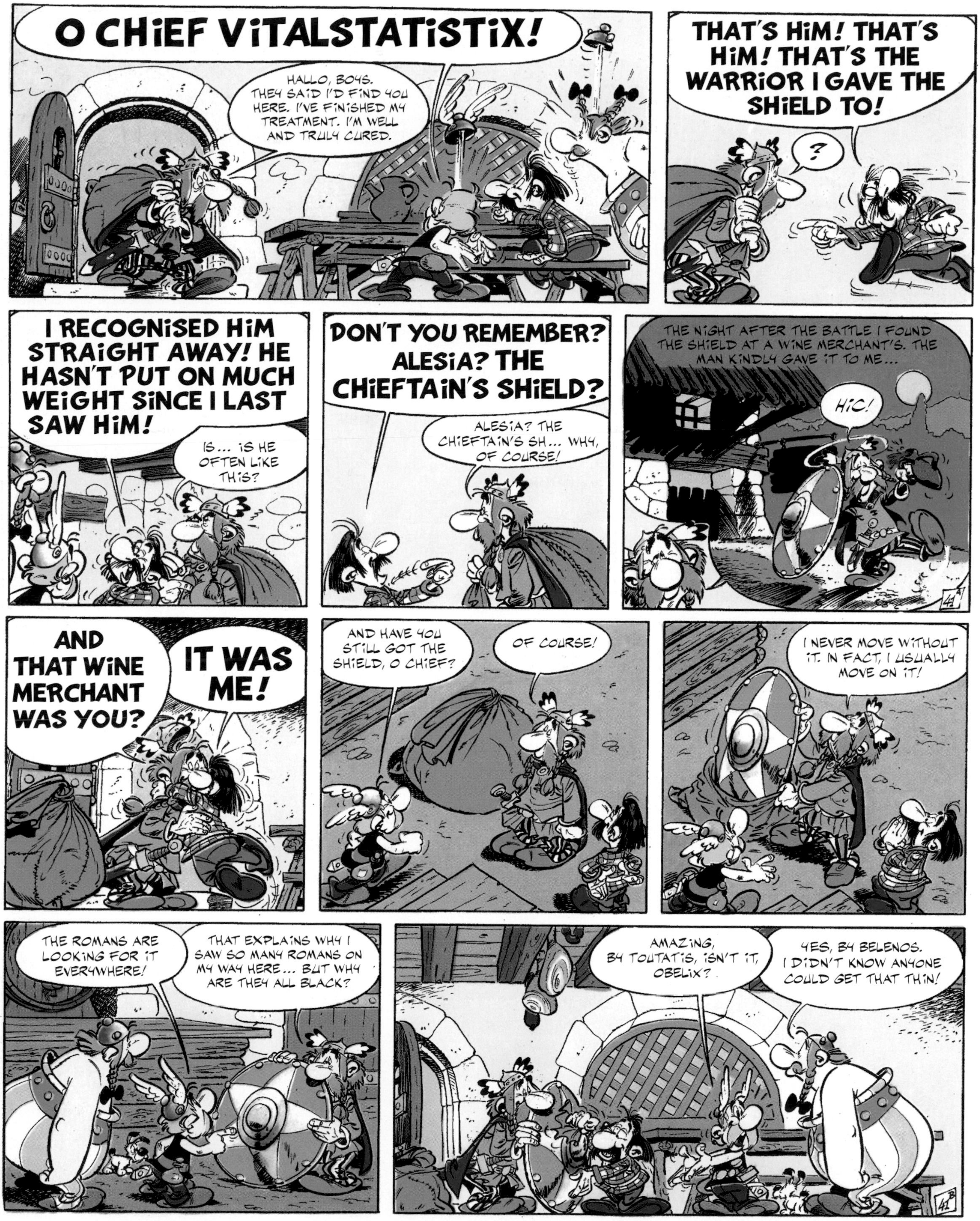
O CHIEF VITALSTATISTIX!
HALLO, BOYS. THEY SAID I'D FIND YOU HERE. I'VE FINISHED MY TREATMENT. I'M WELL AND TRULY CURED.
THAT'S HIM! THAT'S HIM! THAT'S THE WARRIOR I GAVE THE SHIELD TO!
?
I RECOGNISED HIM STRAIGHT AWAY! HE HASN'T PUT ON MUCH WEIGHT SINCE I LAST SAW HIM!
IS... IS HE OFTEN LIKE THIS?
DON'T YOU REMEMBER? ALESIA? THE CHIEFTAIN'S SHIELD?
ALESIA? THE CHIEFTAIN'S SH... WHY, OF COURSE!
THE NIGHT AFTER THE BATTLE I FOUND THE SHIELD AT A WINE MERCHANT'S. THE MAN KINDLY GAVE IT TO ME...
HIC!
AND THAT WINE MERCHANT WAS YOU?
IT WAS ME!
AND HAVE YOU STILL GOT THE SHIELD, O CHIEF?
OF COURSE!
I NEVER MOVE WITHOUT IT. IN FACT, I USUALLY MOVE ON IT!
THE ROMANS ARE LOOKING FOR IT EVERYWHERE!
THAT EXPLAINS WHY I SAW SO MANY ROMANS ON MY WAY HERE... BUT WHY ARE THEY ALL BLACK?
AMAZING, BY TOUTATIS, ISN'T IT, OBELIX?
YES, BY BELENOS. I DIDN'T KNOW ANYONE COULD GET THAT THIN!

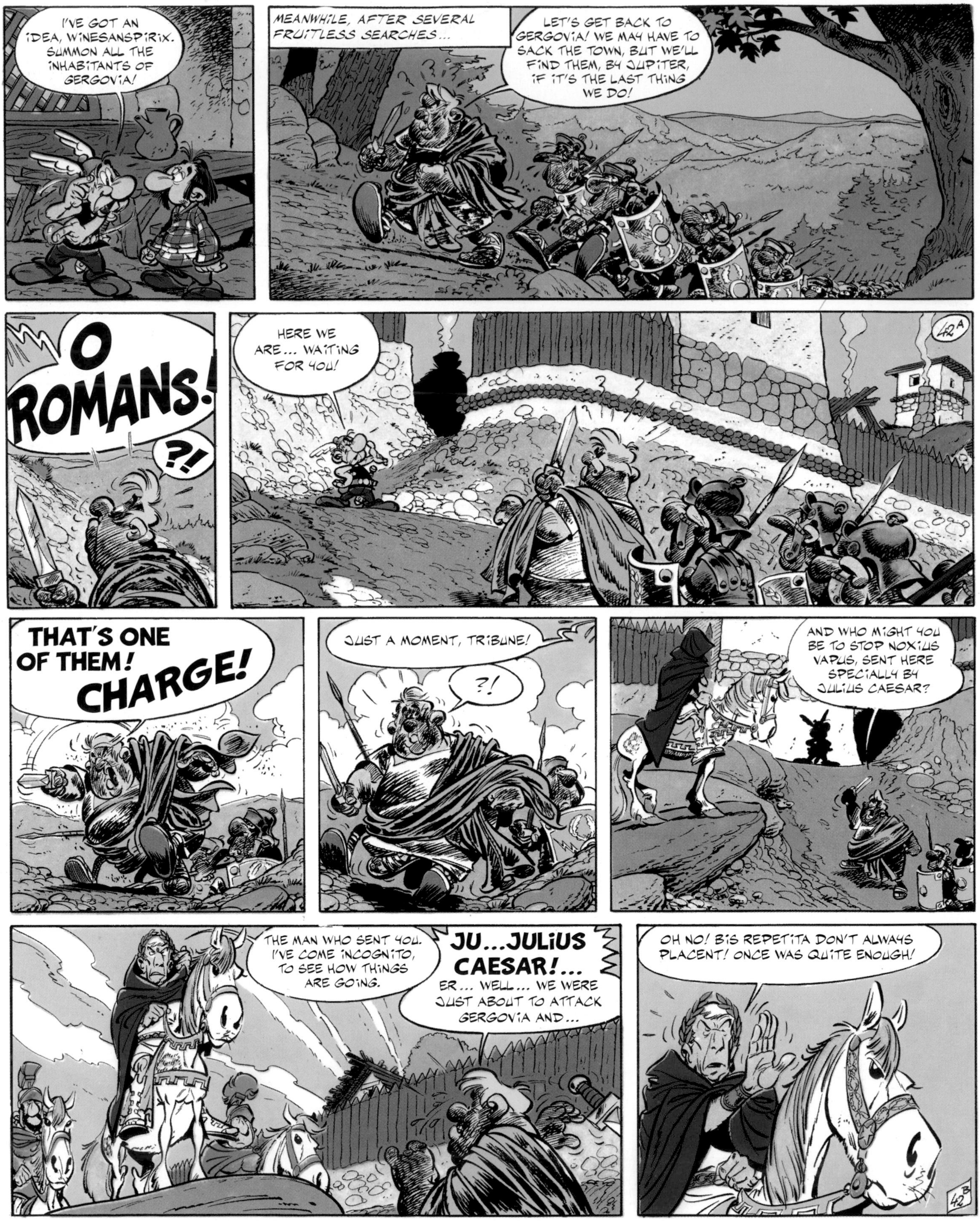
I'VE GOT AN IDEA, WINESANSPIRIX. SUMMON ALL THE INHABITANTS OF GERGOVIA!
MEANWHILE, AFTER SEVERAL FRUITLESS SEARCHES...
LET'S GET BACK TO GERGOVIA! WE MAY HAVE TO SACK THE TOWN, BUT WE'LL FIND THEM, BY JUPITER, IF IT'S THE LAST THING WE DO!
O ROMANS!
?!
HERE WE ARE... WAITING FOR YOU!
42A
THAT'S ONE OF THEM! CHARGE!
JUST A MOMENT, TRIBUNE!
?!
AND WHO MIGHT YOU BE TO STOP NOXIUS VAPUS, SENT HERE SPECIALLY BY JULIUS CAESAR?
THE MAN WHO SENT YOU. I'VE COME INCOGNITO, TO SEE HOW THINGS ARE GOING.
JU...JULIUS CAESAR!...
ER... WELL... WE WERE JUST ABOUT TO ATTACK GERGOVIA AND...
OH NO! BIS REPETITA DON'T ALWAYS PLACENT! ONCE WAS QUITE ENOUGH!
42B

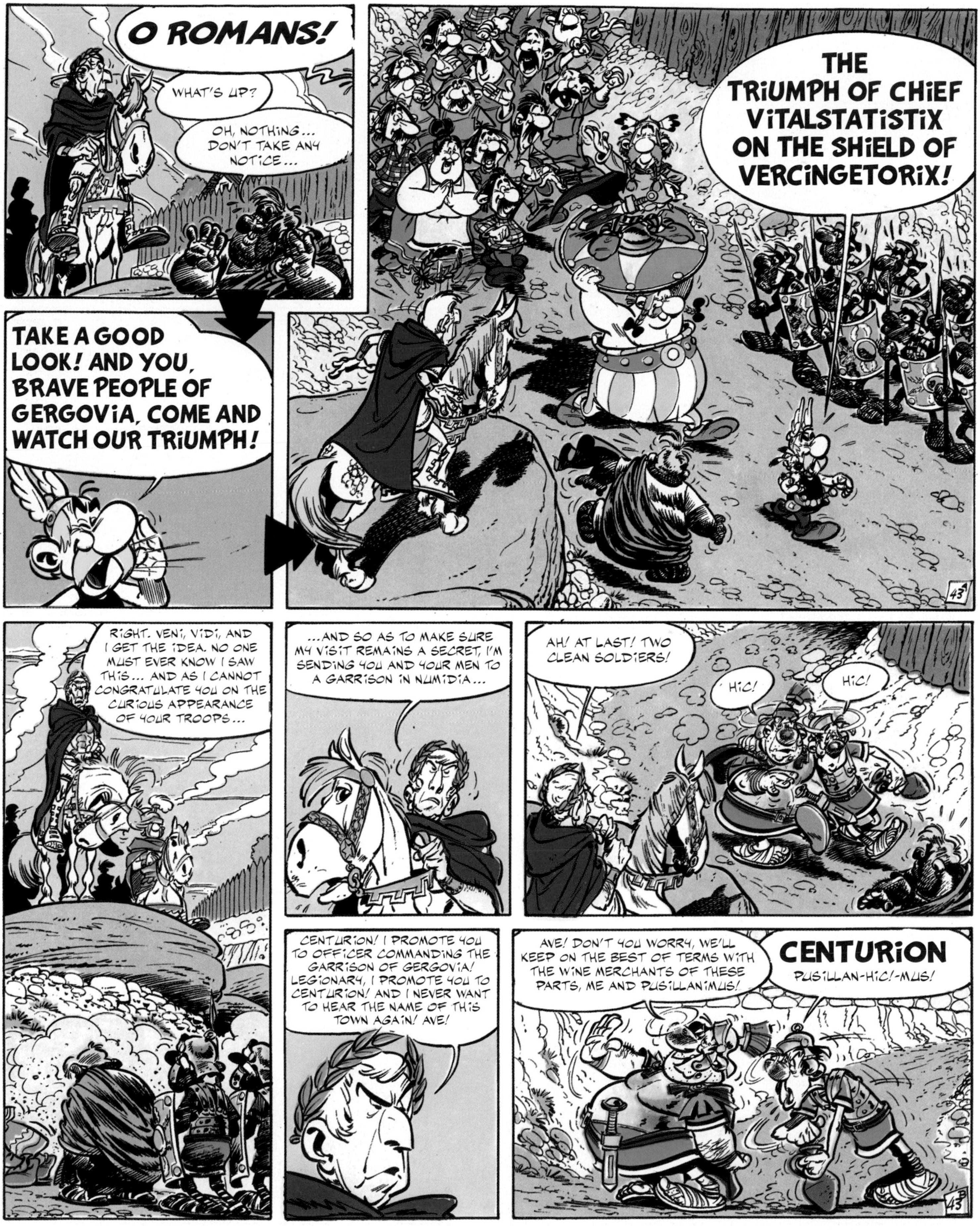
O ROMANS!
WHAT'S UP?
OH, NOTHING... DON'T TAKE ANY NOTICE...
TAKE A GOOD LOOK! AND YOU, BRAVE PEOPLE OF GERGOVIA, COME AND WATCH OUR TRIUMPH!
THE TRIUMPH OF CHIEF VITALSTATISTIX ON THE SHIELD OF VERCINGETORIX!
RIGHT. VENI, VIDI, AND I GET THE IDEA. NO ONE MUST EVER KNOW I SAW THIS... AND AS I CANNOT CONGRATULATE YOU ON THE CURIOUS APPEARANCE OF YOUR TROOPS...
...AND SO AS TO MAKE SURE MY VISIT REMAINS A SECRET, I'M SENDING YOU AND YOUR MEN TO A GARRISON IN NUMIDIA...
AH! AT LAST! TWO CLEAN SOLDIERS!
HIC!
HIC!
CENTURION! I PROMOTE YOU TO OFFICER COMMANDING THE GARRISON OF GERGOVIA! LEGIONARY, I PROMOTE YOU TO CENTURION! AND I NEVER WANT TO HEAR THE NAME OF THIS TOWN AGAIN! AVE!
AVE! DON'T YOU WORRY, WE'LL KEEP ON THE BEST OF TERMS WITH THE WINE MERCHANTS OF THESE PARTS, ME AND PUSILLANIMUS!
CENTURION PUSILLAN-HIC!-MUS!

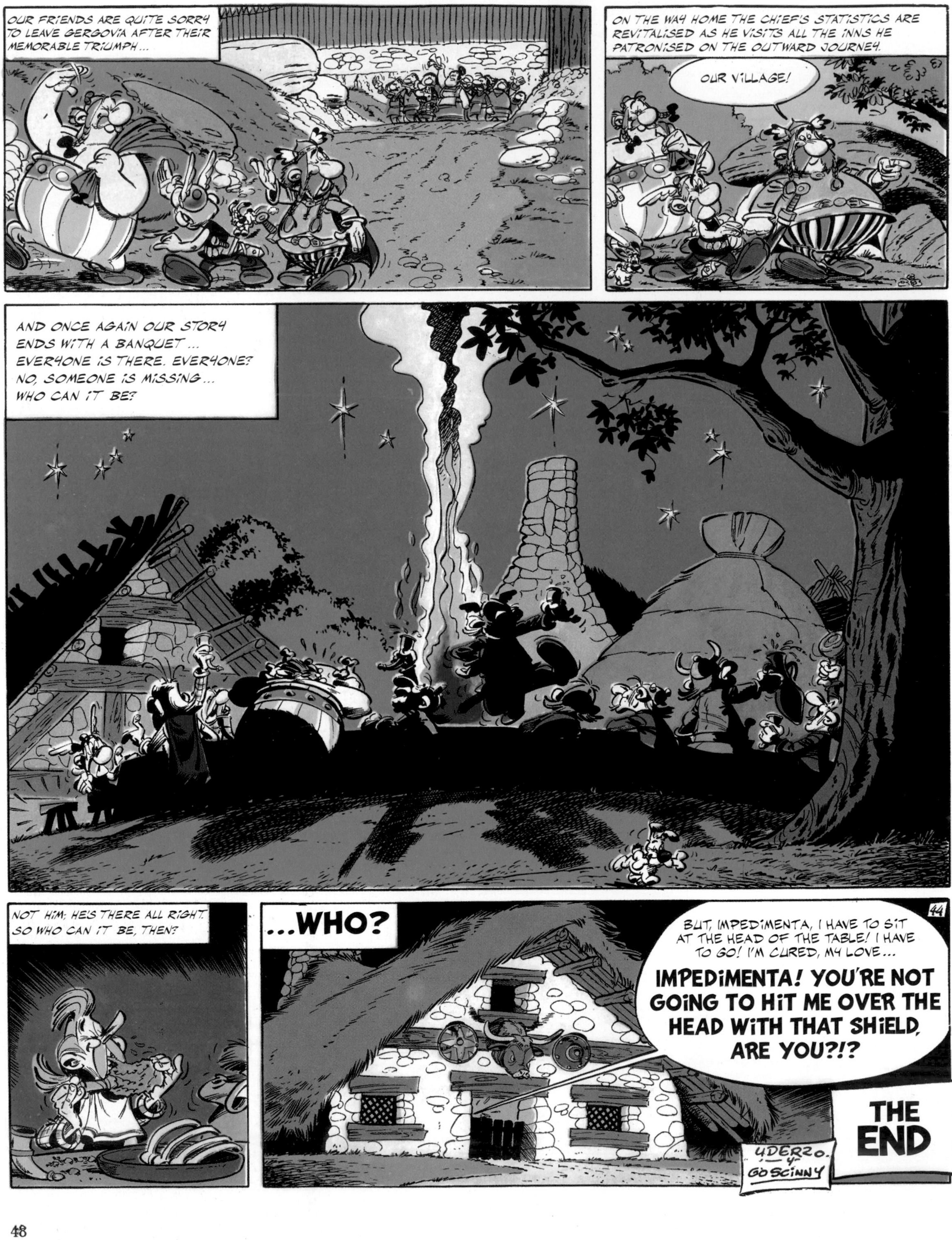

OUR FRIENDS ARE QUITE SORRY TO LEAVE GERGOVIA AFTER THEIR MEMORABLE TRIUMPH...
ON THE WAY HOME THE CHIEF'S STATISTICS ARE REVITALISED AS HE VISITS ALL THE INNS HE PATRONISED ON THE OUTWARD JOURNEY.
OUR VILLAGE!
AND ONCE AGAIN OUR STORY ENDS WITH A BANQUET... EVERYONE IS THERE. EVERYONE? NO, SOMEONE IS MISSING... WHO CAN IT BE?
NOT HIM; HE'S THERE ALL RIGHT. SO WHO CAN IT BE, THEN?
...WHO?
44
BUT, IMPEDIMENTA, I HAVE TO SIT AT THE HEAD OF THE TABLE! I HAVE TO GO! I'M CURED, MY LOVE...
IMPEDIMENTA! YOU'RE NOT GOING TO HIT ME OVER THE HEAD WITH THAT SHIELD, ARE YOU?!?
THE END
UDERZO.
GOSCINNY